Classic City

Lock Down Publications and Ca$h
Presents

Classic City

A Novel by *Chris Green*

Lock Down Publications
Po Box 944
Stockbridge, Ga 30281

Visit our website @
www.lockdownpublications.com

First Edition June 2022
Printed in the United States of America

Lock Down Publications
Like our page on Facebook: Lock Down Publications @
www.facebook.com/lockdownpublications.ldp
Book interior design by: **Shawn Walker**
Edited by: **Jill Alicea**

Stay Connected with Us!

Text **LOCKDOWN** to 22828 to stay up-to-date with new releases, sneak peaks, contests and more…
Thank you.

Submission Guideline.

Submit the first three chapters of your completed manuscript to ldpsubmissions@gmail.com, subject line: Your book's title. The manuscript must be in a .doc file and sent as an attachment. Document should be in Times New Roman, double spaced and in size 12 font. Also, provide your synopsis and full contact information. If sending multiple submissions, they must each be in a separate email.

Have a story but no way to send it electronically? You can still submit to LDP/Ca$h Presents. Send in the first three chapters, written or typed, of your completed manuscript to:

LDP: Submissions Dept
Po Box 944
Stockbridge, Ga 30281

DO NOT send original manuscript. Must be a duplicate.

Provide your synopsis and a cover letter containing your full contact information.

Thanks for considering LDP and Ca$h Presents.

A word from E G

I would like to give a huge shout out to my best friend, my grandmother, a strong woman who always believed in me and a woman who has now passed away and gone to the next life . I would also like to thank my mama Joan and all my old friends who lived in Rolling Ridge back in the day. This has been a great experience working with an author, plus creating a new avenue for myself and my family. I would like to thank everyone that showed me support with bringing this novel to life, and also my children. I've been through a rocky journey with trying to better myself, and this will be the next movement for me to say that I will never divert back to anything other than success. I love all my closest friends and all my supporters. I'm rising, and will continue to as this path builds up more. Thank you.

Acknowledgments

I want to thank Allah for helping me with this passion. I'm striving harder than ever, and I'm hoping to make it last forever. Shout out to Cerenity, my daughter, my mother Dolsellia, my brother Dio. Shoutout to my Muslim brother Dee (Demarcus Armour), Auto (Simeon Slade), (Diantre Hill Tay Tay), my brother Wheat (Detroit Idris Bostic), and my big bro EG (Elmadi Griffith).Thanks for the real friendship.

To all my readers and fans, your love is immaculate. I'm pushing for LDP, for Green Pen Publishing, and Black Spartan Publishing with my best and closest friend (Sunny Giovanni). For my family and all that I stand for. I am Author Chris Green, and I'm working to become the best. Shout out to my cousin Q. Much love. My uncle Kevin Green. All my supporting author friends. My big brother Sa'id Salaam, and every believer that placed an ounce of love or a chance and time into reading my work.

Prologue
Rolling Ridge Slums
Athens, Ga
M.T.

I was sitting in the front seat of my Cadillac Escalade, waiting for the car to appear like a thief in the night. My shooters Freaky and Titty Head were beside me like the two most trusted guard dogs on the turf, and I was itching to use the loaded 45 Kimber that was resting in the grasp of my fingers. I wanted answers, and fast ones, or the east and west of Athens was about to witness why my bloodline was not to be fucked with. I was earning my name in the city for being the boss and straight up guy that everyone known me to be. I dealt fairly with the opposition, but was very strict on the rules of being broke.

"There he go, Marlon. Look like his hoe ass at the light." Titty Head grinned, ready to beat on somebody with the quickness.

He actually spotted them before me, causing my head to look up at this nigga posted at the intersection. Once it turned green, they pulled their way across the street and made it into the back of the grocery store parking lot.

"I wanna know exactly what the fuck is going on, so don't just slap these fools to the concrete until I'm done," I instructed them as my victims came to a halt.

Stepping out of my truck, I dusted off my Polo sweater and lit a cigarette, scanning the area at the same time.

Freaky and Titty Head were on my heels, of course, guns out, so by the time we met with the opposite three, I could smell the fear lingering in the air.

"What's good, M.T. You ready for us? Seven, just like we agreed, big dawg."

Andre was the one speaking first, as if he was the leader of the campaign. I kept my mind focused on not snapping too quick, even though I wanted to break one of their necks like a twig.

"You what's good, my nigga, and these other two lucky guys you got here with you tonight. I got seven uncut and pure baby girls right here for ya." I dumped the bag on the ground, sliding it over with a slight push from my foot.

I was watching the tall dude with the low haircut because his head kept rotating back and forth as if he was waiting for the damn cops to slide in on us. Plus he had already eyed me and Freaky one too many times. Titty Head just clutched on his gun, but didn't say a word

His stare was enough alone. I guess Andre realized that neither one of his companions wanted to check out this batch of my supply, so he approached the bag himself. Before he could even bend down to reach for it, I collided my pistol with his nose, sending him to the ground.

"Shittttt!

"It's a setup!" the tall kid yelled, reaching down for the gun on his waist.

Freaky cleaned him right on up with two shots that startled me for a second from how fast it happened, one to the throat, one to the head. I watched his head open up before he smashed face first into the pavement. Andre's second little ride along watched as the blood poured smoothly from his scalp like ice cream melting off a cone and tried to make a run for it, something that I already knew he would try. I continued to puff on my Newport, looking down at Andre trying to regain his consciousness from wherever I had just slapped it a few minutes ago.

Titty Head chased the second suspect down hastily, knocking him out with a hard right fist. He fell to his knees and caught one slug to the chin before he could straighten his vision.

"Boc!

I watched as Andre shook in horror, witnessing his friends slain in seconds of them arriving. I had to state my message, and I wanted to be crystal clear when I did it. As my two killers walked slowly back over to me, I hunched down, digging into his pockets.

“Let me be frank when I say this, Dre. I like you, but I hate that you ain’t on this side. You an east side nigga, and it seems like some smoke has appeared before my eyes. There was a high school party for Cedar Shoals a few days ago. A girl happened to get raped and murdered. You wouldn’t happen to remember something like that, would you?” I questioned with murder dancing inside of my pupils.

“I never kn-knew who she was, M.T. I left before it happened.” He held his hands in the air, pleading his innocence.

I huffed, noticing that he wasn’t able to speak from being so nervous, so I made it simpler. Cocking back my .45, I tossed the burnt nicotine filter and placed the cold steel to the center of his head.

“Oh God, nooo!” he started to whine before I could even speak my last piece.

“That girl was my baby cousin Aliyah. I’m pretty sure she’s familiar at that school. She’s so precious, like a flower that doesn’t need dirt to grow. She’s gone now, and I need to know who did it?"

He fell loose, lips moving with no sound. Just when I began to grow impatient, he tried to muster up something.

“E.”

My gun roared, knocking a chunk out of the left side of his head. I added two more to his chest before cleaning his pockets faster than a professional contract killer. The darkness covered our identities behind the closed grocery store. It was almost one-thirty in the morning, and not one single vehicle was pushing down the main road.

Tucking my gun, I paced calmly back to the truck. Once Titty Head got behind the wheel, I spoke before any more tragedy erupted from that point.

"I wanna know who did that to Aliyah, and I'll pay whatever to know it all. Make sure y'all slide through Andre's mama crib tomorrow, and introduce y'all selves to a few of them," I said, leaning back into my own silent mode.

"Sho'nuff, big dawg." Titty Head turned up the car stereo before leaving the lot.

I only knew one nigga that had enough hatred to see my blood spilled, one fool that couldn't stand to see a win scratched under my belt. My soul told me not to dwell on it, but my adrenaline boiled every time his name crossed my brain. I knew one thing: if he was involved in any form or fashion, it was gonna be a catastrophe the next time I crossed paths with Stanley Gerald.

Chapter 1
Cedar Shoals High School
7:15 a.m.
Elmadi

It was early the next morning when I got the news of my best friend Andre being slain in the streets like a filthy animal. It was crushing my heart. That was my ace. Coming up from the sandbox, we were impossible to separate. Athens was like the ugliest place to come up when you tried to play around in the hood, a true world of its own. It's the only place I knew that didn't possess love, loyalty, or morals. It was the reason I only rocked with a select few. I knew it would be hard not having my right hand, who had coached me on a lot of shit. I already felt the pressure that was building up behind it, and I didn't want to lose my cool at school after I was so close to finishing.

Sitting outside in the cafeteria outfield benches, I held on to my 380 pistol that I had purchased a week back inside the pocket of my sweatpants. I could feel my finger slowly grinding against the trigger as I pondered on anybody that might have some beef with Andre for any reason. All I could picture in my head was him needing my help, but I wasn't able to assist. My teeth started to scrape against each other, and I sensed my anger soaking freely out of my flesh.

"Are you okay?"

A voice snapped me out of my psych mode. I looked up into Monica's eyes and immediately calmed myself. Her hair was bundled into a ponytail of neat braids. She wore a pair of bleached blue jean Levis that hugged her curves with a matching shirt, and her feet were sporting a fresh pair of Nike Air Max 90s.Her brown skin was glowing to its highest perfection, and her beauty would make a man feel that she was the most innocent woman on earth's ground. She was my friend/girl, with all the right feelings to match, and I was grateful for every moment we was able to rock together. We just had that understandable bond and that respect to know when and when not to violate each other's space.

"Why you sitting over here all alone like this, Elmadi? I know you're grieving. I'm gonna miss him too." She hummed her question and sympathy to me in the same note.

My mind only saw rage a few minutes ago, but her partial sunshine had stormed into my lane quickly. Her energy was just that sweet. "I'm just getting in some thinking time, you know. I live my life staying solid with one best friend, and they took him from me." I shook my head, dwelling on the nonsense.

Hearing the bell ring, I stood up, hugging her waist with a small pinch on the cheek. "See you after school, or at least P.E. With yo' skinny ass," I joked after she walked a distance away.

"Fuck you, Elmadi." Her head swung back and forth like a 1985 chicken head.

True enough, she was ghetto, but still as fine as the next mature, bad thing strolling in the meat market. Her loyalty was intact, and that's the only thing that made a woman perfect in my eyes.

Quickly making my way into the school, I made my way to the twelfth grade hall, smelling the good weed in the air when I passed through the hallway doors. Bitches roamed around doing Lord knows what in the bathrooms. Teachers only taught fifty percent of what we needed to know, and the chances of the students passing the SATs were literally on the floor.

Getting to my homeroom, I was immediately stopped by my teacher.

"Elmadi, you're ten minutes late. Any reason? I thought that I explained to everyone about zero tolerance with being late." Her voice rang with enthusiasm.

I took a seat, taking a deep breath when my eyes crossed over to Andre's seat. I don't know what the fuck had taken place, but I was gonna bet my soul that I wouldn't stop until I found out. I sat back humbly. I wouldn't be from the slums if I didn't.

* * *

The Varsity
(M.T.)
11:35 a.m.

It was crazy that I was riding for my normal pickup during the afternoon. I slid past The Varsity. Not only was it one of the best spots to chow down, it was the main spot for all these stupid-ass niggas that had beef to hang out and get the anger off their chest. I was always careful when I moved, and I've always believed heavily in the hatred that most niggas showed me through actions. It was the reason I did shit with perfect timing. It was to ensure that I always stayed a step ahead.

Toot, a local drug dealer on the east side of Athens, was posted up with a few unfamiliar cats at one of the ordering booths like he was just the boss of all bosses. I still had yet to cross paths with Stanley, but I knew for a fact that his little flunky Toot was bound to have some good-ass info in exchange for his brains to remain inside his fucking skull. The only assistance I had was Titty Head, and that was all I needed.

I shifted lanes, turning swiftly into the eatery's parking lot's drive thru. I didn't want to spook the nigga 'cause he was bound to cause a scene and make a run for it. He was damn sure gonna skate if he seen my face, so I made sure to slow it down as we moved closer towards the group of niggas.

I was out of my whip like a hungry hawk dropping out of the air. He didn't notice me parking my car. My steps were like hops while I inched over to him, and the waitress jumped out of the service window when she noticed me and Titty Head creeping up. I wasted no time shooting one of the men before any of them had a chance to buck.

My strap sounded off loudly, knocking one nigga's brain on the parked car they were standing next to. Titty spotted a man sitting in the front seat of the whip and wasted no time snatching him out and beating him unmercifully with the pistol. As we carried on, earning a crowd performance, I walked slowly over to Toot and stuck my gun up to the bridge of his nose.

"What's good, my boy? You wouldn't have happened to hear from ya guy Stanley lately, have you? Lord knows I'm looking for him." I tapped the steel gently against his skin.

He was breathing like a mule that had been kicking for the last eight hours, and his eyes bulged as if they were ready to pop at any minute. "M.T.., you know I'm solo now. Me and Stanley only see each other while passing in the streets. Nowhere else. That's word. What the hell is the meaning of all this?"

"Damn, that's crazy, because I knew you were gonna say that shit." I rubbed my ear and nibbled on my thumb in frustration.

"How about you give us a different answer out of the box, idiot? Obviously that one is flushed down the drain," Titty Head butted in with aggression.

I was looking around at the people who stood in horror, and it still meant nothing to me. Athens was my town, my spot, and I was gonna make sure every individual standing in my presence at that moment pondered on what the fuck my name was.

"I don't know, man. Stanley is always on the move. Titty Head, y'all know that. But he ain't hiding, and that quote damn sure ain't coming from me. All I know is, I'm not trying to die about a beef that I have nothing to do with. I got respect for both of y'all," he stressed.

I closed the distance between us. I could nearly smell the food he had just eaten rising from his breath. I stared him deep in the eyes, mashing my gun into his face harder.

"You be sure to tell him, and I mean let him fucking know precisely. Pressure is rising in Classic City, so be careful how he ride, 'cause we outside." I mushed him in the forehead before turning to leave.

I nodded to Titty Head. We climbed back into the truck, letting the wheels speak our piece. I had just left another mess on the main street for the Athens PD, and I was gonna continue until the truth was set free.

"Where we headed now?" Titty Head asked.

I was quiet for a moment as I pondered a response.

"Bishop Park. If we see him, or anybody that's close enough to his ass, we handle the business right then and there. I want all of them to sleep like babies," I ordered, tossing the hoodie over my head.

Chapter 2
Stanley G
West side of Athens

I sat back as the stripper from the club last night drained me like I was born to be a faucet. My mental was elsewhere, but she was so fine that I couldn't help but to focus on what was lying in front of me. Raising up my head, gazing at the six-camera monitor, I noticed a car pulling up to my gate on the screen and stopped my action in one motion. Once I locked in on the all-white 1990 Lincoln Navigator, I smiled.

"I'll be back up in like thirty minutes, ma. Just sit back and make yourself comfortable," I said to my little guest before sliding on my clothes and departing downstairs.

If a nigga didn't know who I was, then it would be a good suggestion to ask somebody. At the age of twenty-five, I was a factor in my hood, from the dope game down to the necessary needs in the elderly community around the west and east of Athens. Around the entire city, I held my own when it came to riding, but I had a few shooters from the block, plus enough money to force a family into hiding if need be. Niggas followed me because of the integrity and loyalty I placed behind every action. It allowed me to hold the weight of a true boss, one that couldn't be broken at any cost. I wasn't the average man walking around the Classic City; neither was I invincible. But you was gonna surely know that it was trouble if you pushed me the wrong way, and I remained the champ of that throne still to this present day.

Opening the front door, I smiled. "What it do, my guy? Let me hold some," I joked, allowing my nigga to cross the threshold of my home.

He smirked before replying to me with a brotherly hug.

“I’m still trying to find out how you got all that bread in your bag, big bro. Ain’t nobody doing it better than you on this block.”

His name was Chip Knock, a young hot head from the east side that I dealt with from time to time. Not only was he about his issue, but he was a paper chaser, one that would go and grab the bread by any means. I wasn’t used to dealing with young kids, nor was I fond of hanging and slanging with teens, but I seen something in Chip that I noticed in myself when I was younger. “Money only means something, if you’re using it correctly, li’l bro,” I coached to him as we moved towards the family room of my home.

The decor of my home always placed a chill vibe around my guests, so I was always sure to keep the atmosphere smooth, plus being one of the important dudes out of our spot, I always forced that priceless knowledge down on all my young thugs I had true and genuine love for.

"So wassup, Stanley? Prices looking good, and the business is working in our favor, but we still have one problem that has to be addressed, and to be real, I’m kind of confused on what to do.” He glanced at me with a look of uncertainty.

“And what one problem would that be?” stared into his eyes, slightly confused.

“M.T.., and damn near the entire west side of Athens.”

I’m not a big fan of the whole animosity thing, but I will address the issue if it’s presented. Hearing my li’l homie spit M.T..’s name gave me those nasty chill bumps across my flesh. Hatred wasn’t the word when it came down to the passion we shared about killing one another. I was a boss, and so was he. It just wasn’t enough room for the both of us to keep the streets of Athens on lock.

“M.T. is a smart nigga, Chip. A war right now isn’t smart for me or his business. That’s a mutual understanding with men that's getting some real cheddar. Second of all, I don't give a fuck about that fool and nothing he digging his hands into. I declare peace, but if he steps up to me and my team as if it's anything different...the show must still go on." I shrugged my shoulders with an expression that said I didn't feel any less for speaking down on the gangsta.

"Cool. Also, the car wash business needs a new scrubber in the third car space. The moving rigs are ready to jump out on the road to North Carolina, and I'm guessing M.T. is now on my shit list, so I'll be dipping around with that on my free time, big bro." Chip embraced me with a firm shake, standing to his feet.

I was 6"1", dark-skinned, 200 pounds, and every time I came in contact with Chip, he resembled me in a way. I couldn't say that he was mimicking my style, like he was my son or some shit, but I saw myself inside of the kid when I was younger. I didn't usually spot a beast with the same traits as me, and that alone let me know that he was the next up in line with controlling the block. It was just a matter of time.

"You just make sure you keep your eyes open out there. Things are getting greater, baby boy. I need all my guys that's around me to be eating at a prosperous table beside me. It's like the only traditional street code that's been left in Athens. It's just up to us to uphold it on our end," I explained, giving him the juice to my recipe on how to succeed.

Pointing a finger at me with a smile, he nodded with approval. "That's the reason why you'll always be on top. That good-ass heart. You know for a fact that I got you on my end, Stanley." He shot me the deuces before heading out of my humble pad.

I was now on a five-year run without having a problem in the field. It feel good-more than good. But now I could feel the temperature rising over the game, and I was ready to match any negativity coming towards my way.

* * *

Rolling Ridge Apartments
Elmadi

It was around three o'clock in the evening when I finally stepped off of the school bus in front of my neighborhood. The entire Cedar Shoals nearly stayed out in the east side of Athens, and those were probably some of the most dangerous spots that you could possibly step foot in.

Walking into the front entrance, I noticed Fredreshia, Crystal, and Wanda standing on the side of the first building without a care in the world. Now these females right here were crazy when it came down to giving somebody hell. They all were born and raised in Rolling Ridge and roamed about in a pack whenever they tortured our peace around the complex. As soon as they all spotted me, they didn't hesitate to move my way.

"Hey Elmadi, did you hear about Andre?" Tanya questioned before I had a chance to shoo them away.

She wasn't the prettiest out of all them, but I could probably guarantee that she was the most loyal and stern one that was down to ride forever, remaining that way until the other leaves. We messed around from time to time. Despite the intimate relations, our friendship still carried a championship belt high.

"Yeah, I did, but I ain't really trying to speak on that situation too much right now, girls. But thanks for the condolences." I shot the deuces and continued on about my business.

Once I entered the house, my mama Rosa's voice stopped me in my tracks.

"Hey baby, what's with the long face?" She paused her actions, evaluating me for a second.

I was never good with hiding my emotions, and getting out of the conversation was over when she peeped that my day wasn't going accordingly. She was just that type of mama that was always on point.

"I'm good, Ma, just thinking about Andre. I just gotta find out what happened. I smell something real sour in the air."

She gave me the most worried look ever before taking a seat at the table. "What all do I have to enforce to make sure you stay out of trouble, Elmadi? Because I'm not trying to bury my son. I can't sit around and act crazy like one of these useless mamas that don't give a damn. Andre was involved with the streets, just like you, Elmadi. He was hard-headed, a so-called gangsta by nature. I tried to warn you before any of this turmoil came."

"They took my friend, Ma. How am I supposed to feel about that?"

You supposed to feel exactly how you feel right now, son, but what good will it do if he's already gone? You have to make a new way without him and understand that we only have one life to balance out our days. That's just it, son, and I'm afraid it will never change.

Taking in what my mama said, I bottled up my feelings to make sure she was never able to recognize my thoughts again. My attitude was literally on my shoulders, and she was never gonna be able to switch that up, regardless of what she spilled from her lips.

"I understand, Ma," I replied before heading for my room.

Pacing upstairs to my safe zone, I walked inside, locking the door behind me. My mind was spinning so fast that I only felt one outcome rising from the death of my friend. Death times two. It didn't matter who it fell upon. Some people were about to feel my same pain, and I was gonna be sure it lasted forever.

Pulling my two nine millimeters from the black Nike shoeboxes under my bed, I loaded them slowly and carefully and sat against my bed frame quietly while thinking. I wanted war. I just needed to know who it was gonna be with first.

Chapter 3
Nellie B Apartments
East of Athens
Jameel

It was just another day to me outside of the hood. I was trimming around the east side of Classic City. I had left school early, something I did on the regular if it wasn't no young pussy to chase when it was something I needed desperately. I was taught one good thing fa'sho': never to pull any bull in the hood that I rested my head in, especially when it came down to the Ridge.

After stopping at the gas station and grabbing something to quench my thirst, I made my way inside the Nellie B. These projects was some of the livest over this way and definitely a major spot to come and bump some powder. The crack was recently introduced to the users, and the money flow in the neighborhood started to increase times ten. I had recently started to dab around on my free time and slid down on whatever I could catch before nightfall. It didn't matter who you was. If you were caught after dark, I was robbing yo' ass. Simple.

"Jameel, what the hell are you doing over on this side of town? I'm looking at a real east side hater on my turf," Sky Dog said to me as we crossed each other's path.

We were friends from Cedar Shoals, but most of the time we were out and about, plotting on something devilish for the ultimate come-up. We had our ups and downs, but stuck harder than any nigga on the opposite side. It was also the respect that kept us all on mutual grounds with the real hittas.

"Man, Sky Dog, you know damn well you ain't had no turf or no damn blocks since we were in pre-K, nigga." I smiled, shooting my boy a middle finger.

It was a hot and sweaty-ass day to be walking around Nellie B. The hos were plentiful. There was always constant movement to bring that excitement out to the spot, but as you know, it was never a dull moment for the fuckery to subside in the trenches.

"So what's been going on, Sky? Tell me that you got a move I can jump on and see some dollar signs real quick. Ya boy hungry as a motherfucker, and you know I spazz when I get too damn hungry. I'm trying to make back over to Rolling Ridge before nightfall with a bankroll."

"It's not really much shaking out there today. I'm barely holding my composure," he answered as the Cadillac on chrome Dayton rims pulled smoothly pass us, beating down the trunk with a pair of 12-inch subwoofers. I stared down the whip until it found a space to park

"Who the fuck is that? 'Cause them shiny-ass big wheels shining like my next free pick."

Sky Dog gave me a look as if he wanted to shoot me for even spitting the comment out of my mouth.

"Nigga, that's M.T. Homie like God around this bitch. You might wanna try your best to stay fast away from him if possible. That nigga bad-ass spirit alone will make a nigga cringe up and die. You know it's bad if these fools that's raised out here hustle nothing but nickel sacks when he slides around. He really got the press without being present."

I was listening to all that good info he was spilling, and it didn't matter, not one word. "It sounds like he worth a check if you ask me. I don't have no biased feelings when it comes to whoever getting got."

"He is, and he won't hesitate to put one on your dumb-ass head either for trying something stupid, so I hope you ain't getting no bright-ass ideas through that brain of yours."

Sky Dog's last words pushed clean past my ears, or I just didn't care to listen to them carefully. My mind was one tracked when it came to hustling, and the only thing I could hear at the time was eat. "Say less, my boy. I wasn't really trying to cake up like I'm ya baby mama or some shit. I just came for a small favor. Now that I've found my blessings, I'm sticking around like glue until I snatch them stones off that truck."

"Jameel, I'm telling you, man. Don't go fucking—"

"Just breathe, scary-ass nigga. I don't need a lecture, but homeboy shit most definitely 'bout to need a stretcher." I brushed him off quicker than a track racer.

Pondering on how I was about to pull my mission, I ducked off in Katherine's kitchen to grab a li'l something to eat before I headed back for the hood. The nighttime was just crossing the day out, and I had already made up my mind on wiping this boy's nose like a child.

I slowed my junkie rental down as I pulled back in the Nellie B projects. I made the first right. The Caddy on the shiny rims was still parked and waiting for me, sitting ten cars down. Grabbing my shit, I opened my back door, going in for what I knew. Once I reached the truck, I started to unscrew the first tire, and the rest was history.

* * *

7:30 p.m.
Yacht

It had been over three hours since I last talked to this dumb-ass girl and I was finally starting to lose my patience. Was she in a condo in north Athens? Nah, that's dumb. Hotel? Hell nah, she knows it's probably the first place I would begin to look. My mind couldn't be made up until I came to the conclusion that she had to be with that nigga Elmadi. He was my cousin, true enough, but the family feud that we had going at the time was stacking up to the sky, and it was starting to get beyond frustrating. Her phone rang for the sixth time.

"Hello!"

"Monica, what the fuck, you don't see me blowing you the fuck u?" I barked into the phone

"Yeah, I do, dummy, and you must forgot that I still have a whole nigga. What you trying to do? Crash us out? You need to fall back. Seriously."

I damn near wanted to puke and laugh at the same time. I didn't give a damn about a ho's feelings. Neither was I digging any of the sob shit story to ease my ears. "Monica, you act like me and you ain't been fucking around. I'm guessing its different now because of what day of the damn month it is. Damn, what, you just gon' cut me off, and expect to hide this secret forever?" I shot the indirect threat on the low.

I knew that it was my cousin's Elmadi's baby mama, but I ended up making a slip that was hard to explain. Instead of telling him the truth, I kept the game running until I started getting mixed up in her fuckery. I didn't need Elmadi knowing the truth because I knew it would put a crutch on our family, but most importantly, his relationship. A couple weeks later, I ended up blowing the entire thing out and got the nastiest response ever. He was blowing like a bomb, ready to cut my neck loose, and I deserved it, but I could not help it if me and Monica was physically attracted to one another.

"Are you trying to blackmail me, Yacht? What we did was on some real mistake-ass shit. I wouldn't care what you run and tell anybody, but gotta have a real split between yo' legs if you wanna see Elmadi that mad. You're really willing to expose this weak-ass affair?" she stressed into my ear.

"What she didn't know was the secret was long out, and Elmadi was already shooting the worst of the worst threats, but had yet to expose his hands to her. I only wanted to lock in where I could while I had a chance. I respected the hoe's feelings, and my cousin was more than perfect when it came to his responsibilities. He meant business. But the thought of him chomping me forced my hand to try harder with snatching this bitch from his grasp.

"So I guess Yacht just don't mean shit, huh? Was it that bad?"

"Yes, nigga, it's fuck you, and yes, your little dick sex sucks, nigga. Fake-ass LL cool J!" she shouted into my ear before ending the call

The deceit weighed heavily on my heart, but I was led into temptation, and couldn't shake the power of the V. It just happened to be with Monica.

Using my phone, I dialed a close associate's number. After it rang a few times, his voice boomed through the line. "Yacht, what it do, homie? Why I ain't heard from you?"

"I just been low key, staying out the way. I need a major favor from you, Chief."

"What's that?"

"Set up something with me and E to meet. I wanna squash this shit," I responded truthfully.

"Aye look, Yacht, I'ma be real. You and Elmadi got some real heat boiling between y'all. I wanna stay far away from that." He denied me immediately.

"It's not like that, man. I wouldn't even put you in harm's way like that. I really want to end the shit, at least speak my piece and side of the story. You gotta respect that, Chief."

He was a close friend to Andre's uncle and talked to Elmadi on the regular. All I needed was the chance to explain face to face to bury the hatchet, before our family ended upon burying one of us.

* * *

Athens Police Department
Detective L. Foster

As I scrolled through my file, I located the DNA sample from the night of Aliyah Tate's rape and sent it in for testing. The whereabouts of her killer were still unknown, but a lot of critical evidence was starting to scratch the surface. I knew that soon I was gonna have some names falling across my desk, because the bodies were piling up outside of Athens by the week.

"Hey Foster, you hear what Captain's ordering?" my coworker Johnson spoke loudly as he entered my office.

"What?"

"He needs roadblocks out on the westside today. He's still on the lookout for that suspect, and he's trying to clean it out before we scout for Tate's killer," he informed me briefly.

I nodded, turning back around to my computer. I stared at a mugshot of Marlon Tate on my screen. A true American gangster/thug, if you asked me. I hated to hear his name, but respected the way he moved. He was a hard man to catch, but carried the angry temperament that told me he ran the city of Athens. His demeanor and power proved it. Now that I knew a close one had been slain, I knew he would show his ass sooner or later.

Picking up my office phone, I dialed over to my captain's office.

"What do you need, Foster? I'm busy," he complained before I could speak.

"I just wanted to inform you on the process of the Tate murder, sir. I think it would maybe be a good idea if we sit down with a few students from Cedar Shoals, or maybe call her big cousin in for a few questions on anything he knows." I threw it out there.

I could hear him huffing heavily. "Foster, leave Tate alone. He's clean for right now, and his lawyer is still on the precinct's ass about the dropped gun charge. I need charges that will stick, not assumptions that will lead to a lawsuit on the department for nothing. Be careful with messing around with this dude, because next time we might have to leave him alone for good."

"Sir, no disrespect, but he's only a man, not the Yakuza, Mafia, or the Sicilians. It's just questioning to see if we can get a start." I tried to bait him in.

"You'd be surprised who these people know, Foster. You probably won't find out until your dreams outweigh your death if you sleep on these fucking guys .I'm in charge for a reason, son, and right now, I'm telling you that it's not time. Follow protocol and take your time. Tate's killer will come after. We have a drug-infested city that needs to be cleansed. Get those units on the streets." He ended our conversation quickly.

I tossed down the receiver, staring at the beautiful girl sitting on my computer screen. From my understanding, no one spotted her at the party with an individual, nor did they view her being harmed. It's like she just faded off. But my reality and consciousness as an officer forced me to believe that someone close to her knew more than they were saying.

My brain started to flow, and I started to type a few keys on my laptop. After pulling up the info I was searching for, I picked up the phone and dialed the number to Cedar Shoals high school.

“This is Secretary Williams at Cedar High. How may I help you?"

“Yes, this is Detective Larry Foster from the Athens PD. I must speak with the principal of the school regarding a student that was attending your facility. Aliyah Tate. A child that passed away two days ago.”

Oh yes, sir, I’m aware. Is this regarding her situation?” she asked a second time to make sure.

“Yes ma’am. We have reason to believe that the killer is still attending that school at this time.”

“I’m transferring your call in right now, Detective Foster.”

Leaning back in my seat, I prepared to see a full investigation start in order to see justice brought forth. I knew that I was probably the only cop that was willing to make an effort - a sincere effort at that.

Tossing on my jacket, I holstered my pistol, clipped my badge, and picked up my radio. Exhaling, I shook my head

“I need fourteen units, K-9 squads, and all detectives over to the west side of Athens. I want to start at Lexington Red and swoop the next six blocks with a kid that attends Cedar Shoals or attended that party. Out.” I released the button on my walkie-talkie, giving the order.

Regardless of how much a great cop I was, there was only one thing eating at me. A regular death didn’t occur with Aliyah, and even this Marlon was on my shit list. He deserved justice.

After thirty minutes of checking, searching, and locking up every suspicious person around the Rolling Ridge area, we slid over to Pauldoe Projects. I kicked in a few stash houses and got ahold of some men that we had been trying to locate for years.

Motioning a squad car on the side of me to move forward. my daily smile finally arose when I spotted the idiot inside of the next vehicle.

"Wassup, Li'l Gary? That's what everybody else calls you, right? License and registration." I winked at his nervous ass.

He instantly started to fumble through his glovebox, armrest, even the pockets on his backseats.

"Uh, looks like you must have misplaced them things, huh?"

I already knew that he didn't have any. His name had just splashed headfirst across my desk six weeks ago for an unanswered bench warrant. Aggravated battery on a female. I knew it had to be the jury angel ready to see him, or the little weasel was gonna make my job ten times easier.

"Uh, sir, I think I may have left them in my other work pants, like literally my entire wallet." He smiled with a lying-ass face, as if that shit was about to work.

I snatched the car door open with the quickness, tossing him against it before turning him around. "Put your hands there for me and remain still. You wouldn't reckon to know anything about a young girl named Aliyah being murdered at a house party a few weeks back, would you? Word jumping around is that some of your hoodlums could be responsible. Don't you know that's life in the can if convicted?" I frisked him down roughly.

I tossed him in a pair of cuffs. He was already sweating bullets and trying to toss me his non-negotiating plea. I ignored him for the first fifteen minutes until he said the right sentence.

"Everybody knows what happened to that girl, man. It ain't rocket science. The streets is on blaze about it and shit has went too far," he tried to explain.

I stopped searching the car once the words left his mouth and proceeded closer to him.

"Excuse me? I couldn't hear you. What was that?"

He held down his head before giving the next statement. "I said that you have a war on your hands. A real massacre coming soon, and I don't think you ready for it. Just loosen these cuffs a bit so we can talk, Foster. Please, man, hear me the fuck out."

Walking him over to the cruiser, I pushed him inside the backseat before jumping in the driver's side. Cranking up, I pulled off the scene, heading for the precinct. With my new contestant, I was gonna milk whatever he knew about the recent bull that had my department lines on fire.

Chapter 4
7:45 a.m.
Cedar Shoals High School
Elmadi

I was standing in the field yard talking with Chip Knock the next morning after breakfast. I continuously felt a bad feeling in my stomach. The sun was shining bright and I didn't wake up on the shitty end of the bed. I felt funny, but really couldn't put a finger on it. I just knew something was off. In the midst of me having these thoughts, I noticed Jameel pull up to the school, park, and trail his way smoothly over to us. We stood off to the side with Wanda and Fredreshia before math class, and of course he came over flexing.

He was counting a large bankroll and sporting a new Fila tracksuit. His braids were neatly to the back, and the two new gold teeth he had gotten were sparkling up a storm. A silver bracelet dangled on his wrist, and he rocked a large four karat diamond ring on his pinky.

"Well, if it ain't my people. How y'all living?" He flashed a handful of twenties like he was laying on an ass kiss.

"We alive. But you can put your money away. How'd you get it?"

He folded the knot back into his pocket, folding his arms, just cheesing for victory. "I just did a li'l pick up and drop off and got a bunch of paper dumped off in my hands. I had to go to the east side, but hey." He shrugged, tossing around his poor riddles like it amazed me.

Smiling was becoming my new technique for stupid and clown dudes that fumbled with their lips and the business. I hated to lose money from myself, so my savings alone would crumble his little stash, but I also knew the hood better than a nigga thought. I didn't need anybody scouting my moves, nor did I want anyone to know I wanted Andre's killer but me. Since that was next on the list, I promised myself to play it cool on everybody for a while until I actually knew what was real

"You know, y'all two can come work for me, Elmadi. I'm paying healthy and just launched my own tax service."

"No thanks, Safair Jabari. We alright over this way. We shit paper out like its food. Please find a teacher or something to entertain." I tried to shoo the nigga away. I had too much going on in my mental and he was stirring up even more.

The loud bass speakers coming up the street turned everyone's head immediately. N.W.A.'s "Fuck the Police" was blasting, and once the truck got closer, I recognized that it was M.T. He was driving his money green Tahoe on factories. I watched him swerve smoothly into the school's lot and jump out. In the same instant, I gazed up and Jameel was high stretching it into the school.

M.T. stepped out with a pair of slacks, and he rocked an all-black collar shirt and all black loafers. Two more men stepped out directly behind him The only difference was that they were clutching semi-automatic assault rifles.

Kids started to panic. A few ran for cover, and some were stuck in fear. I moved Wanda and Fredreshia over by a parked Toyota and clutched on the 9mm resting on my hip. Now that I realized the bad feelings were coming to reality that I was thinking about five minutes ago, I prepared myself to shoot one of these nutcases if I had to.

The men moved like they were on a mission, and they looked as if they were heading into the school from how quickly they moved towards the entrance. Before they could reach the doors, the principal, and security of the building stepped out.

Once her eyes noticed the guns the men were carrying, she held up her hands in a declare for peace. I knew it was for the sake of all the teenagers' lives on her plate. "Excuse me, sir, I'm gonna have to ask that you leave this property with the guns. The police are on the way. Now we don't want any trouble, but I can't allow you fellas to go any further." Our principal spoke sternly.

The security was armed and I could see that he wanted to buck for his gun. His life would have been taken before it was pulled or fired, but his bravery was the only thing remembered after he suffered.

I watched M.T. step closer to her and spark a giant Optimo blunt. "I don't care about the police, bitch. I care about your punk-ass student that stole the rims off my car. He attends your thieving-ass school. So I'm here bright and early so a few people can learn. If I'm not mistaken, his name is Jameel. Anybody know him?" He barked loud enough for the surrounding kids to hear on. He looked around at everyone who stood quietly.

"I'm sure that there's a proper procedure that we can take for that. It may not delete the anger, sir, but it surely may get your property back. How about I call the detective and report that he stole your property? If the law can prove it, I'll allow it to rest in their hands, but not the gun." She nodded to Titty Head and Freaky standing next to him emotionless.

"I guess I can make that exception, seeing how many of these wonderful kids came prepared to learn today. We can catch him after school on our own time. I'm positive the school district will be out of his reach. Good morning, principal." He chuckled before making his exit back to his Tahoe.

All three men hoped back inside and pulled off, forcing me to finally breathe. M.T. looked directly at me, but for some reason, he didn't approach.

"All kids, into the school now!" she yelled, rushing us inside.

So many bodies were moving at once, it seemed like the entire crowd was about to fall. After getting inside, we were stationed in the auditorium until we were cleared to leave for the day.

Standing on hold for the next thirty minutes, I ended up crossing paths with Sky Dog. Before he caught ghost, I maneuvered through a few people and tapped his shoulder.

"Yo Sky Dog, fill me in on what the fuck is going on. Did you just see what happened out front?""

"Yeah, you mean Marlon making an entrance up here about his shit being stolen? Hell yeah." He responded like he had a firsthand report on what was about to take place.

"What you mean yeah? That nigga had guns looking for Jameel."

"Exactly. Ask the dumbo why he stole the man's rims off the damn Cadillac, left the man's shit sitting on blocks. They talking about killing that boy, Elmadi. That's just for the disrespect." He explained it to me straightforwardly.

"Is he stupid?

"You answered your own question. Not only that, M.T. has been on a rampage about his little cousin Aliyah dying at Tasha's crib in Pauldoe. Their family is the wrong lunatics to cross. You ever seen the movie *Hostel*?" He looked at me with a crazy-ass expression.

"Yeah, why?"

Because that's the shit they on, and it's real, my guy. People are really hurting women and killing them in our neighborhood. Who's to say you wouldn't have the right to murder someone about your folks coming up dead with no answers?"

That made me pause for a minute, and I was relentless when it came to crafting my own mark in the streets. Plus it was naturally in a male to feel like he could do anything his mind possessed him to, especially in times of a bind. My next big boost was at the newest Polo outlet, and it was right off the exit of the highway, Atlanta 400 to be exact. If I knocked them down for all the material I needed, me and my crew were probably looking at eight grand, maybe ten. I needed the extra money to help Andre's mama with the burial. I also needed to stack up on some insurance and lawyer money just in case.

"Just tell Jameel to be careful, man. I know he ain't perfect, but that fool still grew up on the westside, Sky Dog. Act like it. Make that idiot give that shit back, and slap the shit out of him."

"Alright. Damn, E, I got it, just chill," he assured me as I turned to leave.

"Just don't tell anyone else." I looked back at him so he could see my directness.

I didn't need nothing getting hot on the east side, especially when that's where the grocery spot rested, where my partner was murdered.

"I'm not, E, just relax," he assured me before turning to separate from each other.

The next thing my mind sprinted to was the night of Aliyah's death.

* * *

Two weeks ago
Pauldoe Projects
Tarsha's Graduation Party

I remember tossing back my fourth drink, and I still had Kizzy trying to dance like it was an audition at Mystikal's "Shake It Fast" video shoot. And of course, a few of my exes were there, so I had to keep it cordial when I handled every female. I had a few fun dances with Kim when we first arrived. We chopped it up, but she eventually peeled after bringing up a little too much sad shit that I wasn't trying to hear. Still and all, it was fun.

The house was lit, with decorations and bodies posted on every wall in the room. Weed smoke filled the air, and a few coke heads sat at the tables bumping up lines. My thoughts went to Aliyah sliding past me on the dance floor, moving her hips to some Al Greene. She was looking marvelous Her hair was pinned up into two buns, and her skin glowed like honey on ice. She was fitted into a Valentino backless all black dress and a pair of Guess slides to throw it off. Her makeup was on point, and the mesmerizing black lipstick she wore kept the entire room's attention with every step she took.

A few loud-ass guests arriving fucked up my entire focus. I noticed it was Kevin, Freaky's little brother, and Onyx, along with a lot of niggas that went to Clark Central high school. I decided to sit back in the dark, watching intently. I was keeping my cool, but I knew at any time one of these grown-ass fools could get out of line, making a whole episode in the spot.

Eventually the music slowly faded. Guests started to lessen, and the thick crowd had turned into an empty and filthy, wrecked home. I didn't waste any time picking up a broom. Something made me start in the bedrooms. I opened the bathroom door inside of Tarsha's sleeping area. My eyes landed on Aliyah, beaten horribly, with her clothes scattered across the floor. She was covered in blood, but alone. Dropping the broom, I kneeled down beside her, scared to place my hands near her wounded face to see if she was breathing.

Jumping to my feet, I broke to the front room, telling Tarsha before making my way out of the front door. I was so drunk that I could barely recognize that it was her, even after our last encounter no more than three hours prior. I released the vomit sitting in my stomach before getting in my car to peel off. The next thing I knew, I was waking up to my mother's television blaring the death of a seventeen-year-old at a reckless house party. It's the only thing that slammed into my ears after the nasty sight flashed back through my head and eyes.

Snapping back into reality, I pictured every face that stepped inside of that home, and the guilty suspect slithered right into my consciousness.

Chapter 5
1:34 p.m.
Westside of Athens
Toot

After dropping my baby mama Tanya off at work, I stopped at the closest Checkers in the neighborhood to grab something to eat. I had two drop-offs to go and had to load up my workers with four zips a piece and finish it off with a Mary Jane to my main clientele, Chip Knock. He always spent a rack or better, and that little change was exactly what I needed at the time.

After grabbing my food out of the pick-up window, I pulled towards the lot, and my car was quickly blocked in by three Lincoln sedans. The windows were too tinted, so I couldn't see a thing. I played with the gas pedal to see if the bitches would budge, but I had no luck.

After a minute of me brainstorming, I watched Li'l Jermaine from the westside step out from the backseat of one of the cars. The grin that he gave said that we weren't cool. He had a P9 semi-automatic rifle in his hands. I wanted to remain calm, but my heart was thumping out of my chest, and my paranoid-ass face was obviously giving me away.

A few more stepped out of the other cars and proceeded towards me, and I rushed to reach for my snub nose .38 under the seat, but ended up raising my head to a long barrel sliding under my nose. Jermaine was snarling at me like an angry pit-bull, ready to pull trigger and kill me. I knew it just from the stare down. He wouldn't even blink.

Jermaine was a young dude out of the hood that killed a nigga at a house party when he was fourteen. He had been on the run since, but now I was hearing the feds was on his bumper. He was now seconds away from blowing me a new

Botox lift, and once I spotted Stanley Gerald step from the passenger side, I knew some serious shit was in effect.

Opening my car door, he sat directly in the passenger like we were best friends. I sold packs for him, true enough, but a personal relationship was never established, only business.

"My nigga Toot. Just checking in with you. Anything nice for me?" he questioned, checking out his beard in the mirror.

"Yeah, yeah, bro, is something wrong? Like I was gonna get at you today. Am I late or sum?" I asked, not really knowing what was on his mental.

"Nah, my nigga, it ain't no problem." He smiled, taking the roll of money from my left pocket. I just need to ask you something.

"What's that, Stanley?"

"Why am I hearing about you speaking on my schedule across the phone? Chip Knock said it sounded like you were giving someone the plans to my entire day the afternoon you stopped by the spot. You don't know about any beef or plots scattering around about me, do you? I mean, I'm just asking to make sure?" His thick voice demanded an answer.

I stared over into his satanic eyes, feeling his energy like a heartbeat. His jawline was twitching, and he started to nibble on the end of his thumb while twisting his ear, something he always did whenever irritated. Knots started to turn in my stomach.

"I just wanna be straight on something, Toot, 'cause you know that we've had major understanding with each other since all this shit began. I've treated you well since the start of our dealings. Lately, I haven't been feeling the same myself, so I pray that I'm not about to be crossed no time soon. I don't need a snake in my grass, 'cause right about now, he might get everybody around me cut in half like a break line." He clamped his fingers together like a pair of scissors.

"I've rocked right since day one. You ain't gotta think like that with me, never." I shook my head, wondering what he was about to do next.

We were holding the Checkers parking lot up with traffic, and I could see the employees scrambling around the small box as if help was being contacted.

Stanley smiled at me and started to pop his knuckles. The next words he spoke were through clenched teeth. "If I find out you're committing treason and working with the other side, Toot, I'm gonna split you in half with a fucking chainsaw. Nobody in Georgia or Athens will ever find you. You're gonna be cranberry juice for a pig's pussy. You hear that?" He touched my temple twice with his index finger.

Sucking up my weak-ass pride, I took that disrespect on the chin as he stepped out of my car, slamming the door behind him. He paced coolly back to his tinted-out Lincoln and jumped inside. Jermaine was still holding the gun to my face, and I was being sure to not to buck and catch his free slug of the day.

Removing the gun from my face, he aimed at my tire, blowing it out.

Rubber scattered through air, forcing me to jump. I could smell smoke after the first few seconds. I expected more than one round to release, but when I peeped out of the window, Li'l Jermaine was ducking inside the car, swerving out of the lot recklessly.

My heart was beating so fast that I didn't even know I still had my car in drive. Moving hastily to get out of the citizens' way, I pulled out of the restaurant on a bare rim, scraping the concrete at forty miles an hour. I was only known for getting a little dough from here and there, so I didn't know what the hell Stanley had going on in his brain, and I didn't need another incident like this one to make me understand this fool was retarded. Those were shoes that I couldn't fill.

I knew two things were guaranteed. I was gonna find the slime ball that mixed my name in the filthy-ass statement that I just heard, and I was gonna hand they ass straight over to the wolves the same way they tried to do me. I knew how niggas got down in Classic City. I was gonna cross before I got crossed.

Chapter 6
Jackson-McWhorter Funeral Home
Aliyah's Wake
M.T.

After viewing my little cousin's Aliyah's body, I cried my entire heart out until there was no tears left to drain from my eyes. My entire family had dispersed, none giving me any insight on something that could have put me closer to her killer. I scanned every kid that came in who attended Cedar Shoals. I was missing so many pieces that I was nearly about to wrack my brain on who to kill next.

My phone rang, and I didn't hesitate to answer it.

"I'm listening."

"Marlon?" My sister cried through the line silently. I could hear the sniffles every time she breathed. "Have you found anything on Aliyah yet? Have the cops heard anything?" she asked in desperation.

As much as I wanted to end our painful saga, I had to be upright and truthful when it came to the family and our business. "No sis, not yet, but people are talking, and I'm close. I'm not sleeping until whoever did this burns, baby girl. That's word to Mama." I closed my eyes, envisioning the torture I would cause once I got ahold of them.

"I know that it's not gonna be your first priority every second, but remember that these people took your niece away from me. I can never have her back, Marlon, so you shouldn't care how you act out against these people. I'll be sure to call you if I hear anything," she grieved, before ending the call.

I exited the funeral home. I had gotten word to meet Chip Knock at the nightclub for an update and drop-off. I timed the nightfall perfect and made it across town just when shit was starting to wake up.

It was around ten when I pulled up into the spot in the corner where Chip sat at a personal table, waiting humbly. It had been a while since I been to the V.F.W., but I was surely a known face around the way.

"My young'un, it's a blessing to see you today. I see you still doing what you do best."

I sat down, sliding the four way across the table. I was ignoring the music and extra bullshit that was going on around us. I was too focused on him to see if the feelings that I'd been having lately were just me tweaking.

"I'm good, M.T. It's always a blessing to be around my guy."

"That's right. Check this. I need a little insight on something. Has anything strange been occurring lately - death threats, or some foul shit being said?"

"Bro, niggas talk about you daily. I've been hearing shit since I've met you. You know niggas hate." He smiled.

"That's always facts. But lately it's been a lot of real snake shit sliding around the Classic City, my man. I mean, you're a hustler that migrates from the west side to the east faithfully. Do you think there's been any tension floating around?" I threw the question back in the air to see how he would react.

"Besides the animosity between my two baby mamas, hell, same ole Athens. Why you ask that?" He gave me a curious look.

"I don't know. I've been getting a lot of bad threats and calls. Indirect-ass stuff. People who claim to give info, say that it's coming from Stanley G."

Chip spazzed out into a fit of laughter as if I was just nominated for the best joke of the year. He waved me off like I was insane, so I just played it off and allowed it to slip to the back of my mind. Just when I started to relax, I looked at the entrance, spotting the snail himself coming across the floor up to the bar.

"I gotta be back. I'm going to take a piss," Chip stated to me, pulling off in a hurry.

Still and all, I didn't flinch from my target. My Glock 17 was ready on my hip, thanks to my nigga Red, posted at the door. I was strapped harder than a car seat.

Standing up to my feet, I tunneled in on him and his four associates that stood guard beside him like the walls of a castle. My head already told me to shoot them all and be done with it, but the street code and truce had been pushing for decades on the same blocks that we were raised in. Trucking through the crowded floor, I caught up with Stanley in a small personal section. We weren't no more than twenty feet away from each other.

"Yo, Stanley?"

His head turned, mugging me with nasty envy. Tooting up his nose, he tried to walk off with no response, and that wasn't good enough for me.

"I asked for your time because I called your name, my nigga. Maybe you need to cut the disrespectful shit and pump your brakes to see what the fuck I want. Common respect would be for you to hear me out, nigga, "I said over the dense music.

He paused, facing me with a retarded grin as if I was talking to the jacket on his back. "Maybe I wasn't even trying to acknowledge you, my man. I'm in my own smooth lane, ya feel me? So if you don't mind, I'll be sliding, jack." He turned his Kango to the side arrogantly.

"Word is you holding some beef with me on the land. I hope that's just mist in the air. You know how these stupid-ass fiends and junkies can get. Start slanging issues all around the city, getting bullets flying everywhere." I looked him deep into his face, showing him the death crawling on my body.

"If I had any problem with you, these good dudes right here that I call my guards would've probably been shot you in front of the whole damn club, sucka! I'm having fun, so how about we just relax, 'cause we will see each other out there.'

His remark bit my soul. I had a feeling he knew what happened to my little cousin Aliyah. I was damn near sure of it. Pulling the Izod hoodie over my head, I trucked straight towards the entrance. I never let my people know what was up because I was officially about to rock buddy's ass to sleep. I was wasting my time, and also losing money in the process with the police watching my every move.

Making it outside, I jumped in the driver's seat of my baby blue Mercedes Benz. Reaching under the seat, I grabbed the loaded Mac 90 automatic and started my engine. I drove off smoothly, making sure I wasn't being trailed. After my eighth red light and seventh turn, I knew that I was okay. My prayers and thanks were surely with God for me holding my anger, because the next time my two pupils landed on him, I wanted to see blood. Lots of it.

* * *

Rolling Ridge Apartments
11:30 p.m.
Elmadi

It was starting to get later on in the night, and my mind kept thinking of the mission I had at hand for the rest of my evening. Me, Vida, Crystal, and Joy were the only four left, hanging out in the Ridge like it was a twenty-four-hour game room.

My phone started to ring, and Kim's name begin to flash across the screen. It was crazy how she called on time, 'cause these were the moments where her words soothed me the most.

"Hello?" I picked up quickly, hoping to catch her.

"Hey Elmadi, I appreciate yo' big head self for calling me. I been at my distant family's house for the past three weeks, and you ain't picked up not once to hear my voice, huh?" she questioned with sadness in her tone.

"Please, love, you know it ain't no me without you, plus I stay ready to choke you, so I be needing this time to control how I contain you." I laughed into the receiver to spread some brighter energy.

"You silly, boy. It's been on the news about the foolery every day, and I really wanted to just check on you. I know your mind can wander off sometimes."

It was crazy hearing her say that to me with the shit I had to pull within the next two hours. I didn't know if it was my sign not to go, or more push to handle the business. I cherished the fact the we were first loves, and she still showed an unconditional amount for me. It only proved to me that we had a true, real connection.

"I know, it'll be okay." I leaned back on the brick wall behind me.

"Nah, you won't be okay until you move away from the crazy-ass detention center you live in. I keep telling you, E, it's the only way that anybody from there even put the word achieve into perspective. You have to be you, think different, and make your own routes. That's what this is all about." She panted on the line.

Knowing she was finna pull one of them mushy-ass stunts, I had to go ahead and end our little late night greet. "I love you, Kim, but I gotta call back tomorrow. Think of me like I do you." I hit her with my normal sweet line like usual.

"Who the fuck are you talking to?" Monica's voice popped out of nowhere.

I glanced behind me, and she was posted in my doorway like she paid my Mama's bills. Hanging up the phone, I stormed over to her and jacked her silly ass in the crib, slamming the front door behind me. "You must don't remember the message in my Mama's home. Respect it how you want to be respected."

Hearing me speak that shit, she slowed down and got quiet. "You started it. You outside hanging out with these little cunts and talking to God knows who. Just tell me you don't need me here and I can leave, Elmadi."

She mushed my head and continued up to my room. After a few seconds of her bipolar shit, I took the authority on acting out first. Bomb rushing her crazy ass in the room, I slammed my bedroom door. I dunked her face first into the sheets and started to shred her clothes.

"Fuck you, E. You think I don't know about all them hoes, huh? You a psychic player, let you call it. You tryna hide these bitches like I don't know. Nigga, you ain't got no respect for me." She pouted with them fake-ass tears that I wasn't buying.

Stripping her from head to toe, I prepared myself to do the only thing capable of snatching her tension, to show that love the one way that no other man couldn't.

* * *

After finishing my make-up session with Monica, I called my cousin Vida, loaded up my two nine-millimeter pistols, and jumped into the rental I grabbed earlier that day. We were heading to the east side of Athens - Pauldoe Projects to be exact. I had ended up getting word about a cat named Johnny, a young hustler that attended Clark Central High, mixing my name into some bullshit with Andre's family. After he was murdered, it was said that I allowed him to head to east side of Classic City right into an ambush. Now my mind was on the true fuckery, because Andre's mom, and pop knew me since I was a kid, and that was probably about the only reason they still allowed me to even speak my voice on anything dealing with my best friend.

It was pitch black and nearly going on one-fifteen in the morning when we entered the apartments.

"Pull the car over there, Elmadi. Don't park right in front of the building." Vida coached me as he held on to the Colt 45 automatic handgun.

"I got it, I got it," I assured, not trying to get my adrenaline pumping too hard.

The apartments was nearly empty besides the movement that was going on around the twenty-four-hour trap spot that was run by Johnny's uncle, a known killer that was plugged in with Stanley Gerald on the illegal tip.

Parking the car, we both climbed out of the car, guns in hand, and found our way to the edge of the building. My eyes were trained on the front door of these niggas' crib. I didn't want to run in and take what they had, nor did I want to annihilate the kids or innocent people. I only wanted Johnny and that shit was stamped.

"Elmadi, I don't need you blanking out and doing the most. When this nigga come out this spot, we handle it and leave. Understood?" Vida asked, pulling the chamber of his gun back.

"I told you I got you, Vida. Shut the fuck up talking and let's handle it." I kept my eyes focused on the prize.

Just when he was about to make another statement, I watched the door come open, and sure enough, Johnny came trailing out the door all sluggish like he'd smoked a bag of weed or something. It was the usual time he left his uncle's trap, and it must have been God for us to be there at the perfect moment to handle the business. Once I spotted the door close behind him, I looked at my cousin. He remained quiet, but gave me the nod, and I was moving like lightning with him directly behind me.

As we ran down on this fool, I could feel my heart thumping harder than a speeding train. He didn't see us, nor did you hear a sound under our feet as we crept across the soft grass.

By the time we got closer to where I could aim my gun, this man turned around and locked eyes with me, as if a text message had just alerted him of what was about to happen. His pupils widened like a deer in the headlights and my finger was wrapping around the trigger at that same moment.

"You made the wrong mistake mentioning me to that idiot," I said as my first bullet fired off and ripped through his cheekbone.

His grunts were silenced with another two bullets from Vida's pistol. The shots were so loud that I even noticed a few lights cut on from the surrounding apartments. I saw Johnny's body twitch, and I ended it all with another slug to his face.

"Let's go." Vida grabbed my arm, snatching me back towards the car.

I could feel my stomach turning knots with every step we took, and right before I jumped into the driver's seat, I hurled right in the middle of the street.

"Man, what the fuck? You getting weak, nigga. Let me find out this your first time!" Vida slapped the car door repeatedly.

Flicking him a bird, I climbed into the driver's side and smashed off. It was crazy because truthfully, it was my first time pulling the trigger to a gun on another man. The only thing that gave my finger that extra pressure was Andre's life, and I would do it again if it led me closer to the man that I needed to deal with next.

Straightening myself up, I jumped on the expressway and glanced over to see Vida's pissed expression.

"You can feel how you want, but this shit will keep going like this, and I'll be puking a thousand more times until I figure out what the fuck happened to Andre. So regardless, you stuck with me. I need your help, 'cause you the only one I trust," I stressed to him.

"I got you, Elmadi. Just remember what you asked for," he huffed, leaning back in the seat.

Chapter 7
Georgia Square Mall
10:30 a.m.
Elmadi

I had been posted outside of the Georgia Square shopping mall for at least the past hour. Two men out of my crew were waiting patiently for my calls inside the selected stores as potential buyers. There was a new Adidas outlet, plus the Ralph Lauren section. Now all the prices of my sweep licks were usually sweet, and it always went smooth. A five-man crew, three cars, and a couple of people spinning the lot in the same cars for our decoy to make a clean getaway. I had spotted Athens PD probably about once since we first started our prowl.

"E, why you just don't push the button? It ain't gonna be no better time than this?" Eric asked impatiently.

He was one of my main snatchers, but today I was short a wheel man, so he was the next in line to whip us up outta the mall and head back for Rolling Ridge.

"Because, this is a ten thousand dollar move. We need this, and I damn sho' didn't pull all the way down here to Georgia Square for a failed mission. We ain't moving until Stacy and Vida pull up with that third set of wheels." I shut his idea down quickly.

Just as the sound of his huffing dribbled across my earlobes, I snapped my head to the side, noticing Stacy's Dodge Intrepid come to a screeching halt beside my car. He was smiling all thirty-two at me like his ass wasn't forty-two minutes late for a whole cash cow.

Rolling down my window, I shook my head at his dumb ass. "We're looking at about ten minutes. Grab everything you can as if this will be our last time," I ordered.

"Enough said."

Using my cell phone, I speed dialed my next snatcher in charge.

"Are you ready? I'm sick of pacing around this bitch?" He picked up quicker than I expected.

"Go take off! You got five minutes," I said before hanging up.

Eric, Stacy, and Vida were hopping out of the cars on my cue, making their way into the mall's entrance. I kept my eyes alert around the area, because I knew the cops wouldn't hesitate to appear like Houdini. I didn't need shit happening out of thin air and costing me ten thousand dollars' worth of merchandise, plus a trip to jail was not the way I needed shit to end.

After a minute of tapping my foot repeatedly, I watched my first two boosters fall out of the mall doors with a hand full of denim jeans and Polo shirts. A large smile spread across my face when I witnessed the last two bust through a couple in front of them to get out of the building. Vida and Stacy were also on their heels.

I watched closely and calmly as they loaded up all three cars and started to pee out, one by one. Once my two boosters loaded up my backseat, they were diving in on top of the load and my feet was mashing the gas. I watched Stacy flick me a bird before doing the dash out of the parking space. Once I knew we were all in the clear, I was smashing straight for the intersection

"That shit was sweet, but we had extra security in there today. It's like they knew we were coming!" Eric informed me as he looked in the rearview repeatedly. "Shit might get sticky."

"How many loads did they get?" I asked, trying to add up the profit in my head.

"If everything fell perfectly, we struck for about seven loads, and that was just only the number I seen with my own eyes. At the most eight," Eric assured.

Before I could reply, the sound of a police cruiser pulling up behind me forced my eyes to shoot up at my rearview.

"Aww shit, we got a couple of friends trying to kick it with us. You might wanna put on your seat belt if you ain't trying to be in the county on a work detail by this time next month." I glanced over at Eric seriously.

"Man, you need to floor that damn pedal and get us back to the westside of Athens. I'm not about to get slammed for some apparel that I ain't even put on my ass yet."

"Just sit the fuck back and let me work, nigga. I got this shit. Just make sure you don't fall out of the car seat, crybaby-ass boy," I joked, making a hard right turn.

The one thing I knew I was official with was working that wheel of a car like a speed racer. My skills had been up to par since I was about twelve, and I definitely wasn't about to let Athens PD catch me. I watched the authorities snap around the same corner, trying to keep up with the Dodge motor under my hood. Watching a second cruiser appear from my peripheral, I straightened up in my seat like the letter L and prepared to speed it up a bit.

"Uhhh, E, that light don't look like it'll be green by the time we get to it, bro!" Eric shouted with worry as I smirked, gazing up at the approaching intersection flooded with traffic. "Don't do it, Elmadi!"

He was yelling in my ear like a hooker being smacked to the bed, but my mind was focused on making it home.

"I'm doing it!" I mumbled back.

The color on the light turned yellow, forcing me to speed it up a tad. By the time I was crossing the lane and the first squad car accelerated behind me, he was smashing directly into the side of a civilian's car. The loud crash grabbed my attention for a slight second, but I quickly regained focus, placing my eyes back in front of me.

"Shittt!" I cursed with a sympathetic face as I busted a hard right on the next street.

Knowing Athens as well as I did, the helicopter and reinforcements was surely on the way, but I wasn't gonna give them any chance to make their job any easier. Boosting was just a minor lick to what I had on my list. It was just a start with the merchandise we got today. It was eventually going to rise to money, jewelry, and maybe even a few paintings if I could move the hand quicker than the eye. Two of my crew members turned onto the Atlanta highway.

I knew in my head that it was just the beginning. I just wanted to maintain until Andre's killer resurfaced back up for me. I wouldn't be able to rest my mind until the chapter closed indefinitely.

* * *

Detective Foster
Clarke Garden

Since I had been investigating the recent bodies dropping on the east side of Athens, I located bundles of information that was leading me closer to the person I needed to place behind bars for the rest of their natural life. The morning wind was thick as bear skin, and the negative aura from the infested neighborhood still had me on edge despite the sun sitting high in the sky.

I leaned forward in my driver's seat when I noticed the all-white BMW pulling out of the complex. It didn't take me long to spot my man through the crystal-clear windshield. As he made his way to turn out, I hit my siren lights, jumping directly behind him. I thought that he would probably give me a good chase, so I placed the cup of coffee in my hand down. To my surprise, he immediately started to slow the vehicle down as soon as I hit my flashers.

Rising out of my police cruiser, I slowly walked up to his driver's side door, hand resting on top of my pistol just in case the animal inside of this monkey-ass thug started to get belligerent. Using two fingers to tap the glass, I watched as it rolled down slowly.

"What can I do for you today, Officer? Don't look like I violated no law, if I'm not mistaken. You wouldn't be just bothering a big ole boss like me on the strength, now would ya?" M.T. asked with a conniving smirk.

I knew the man that I was standing in front of at that moment was far more than dangerous. He was menacing. His smooth, innocent look would trick the most, but a three second glance at his criminal record, and most would try and make it to the closet place of safety. He was a gangster - one that damn near couldn't be touched.

"It's a great day out, Mr. Tate. Condolences have truly been on my mind for your little cousin Aliyah. I've been pushing night and day to search for her attacker. I was just really wondering, have you found put anything new? The department could really use as much help as you can find," I asked to see where his mind was.

I had already questioned a few rats that portrayed to be gangsters, ones that didn't have the heart to serve a year in a prison cell, and came up short each time. These were men that were willing to give up any kind of information to stay free, even it had to come with a lie.

"We haven't heard anything that the slow-ass department of Athens haven't heard. I mean, come on, let's be real. A motherfucker raped my seventeen-year-old cousin. I damn sure don't think he'll be turning himself in no time soon. I don't even see these sorry-ass officers trying to go track the fucking murderer down. Guess that leaves her as a cold case," he replied back to me with the slick comment.

"It has been getting king of cold out here, but that's not the case, Marlon."

"You can just leave it as Mr. Tate."

Forcing myself not to reply with stupidity, I humbled my thoughts. "I know that the death of a family member could be critical, Tate, trust me. I'm not trying to be an ass, I swear, but the concrete under Athens, Georgia is bleeding your name with all the pandemonium and fuckery that's taking place. I'm no genius, but I can bet half of those dead men caught a bullet from a mad heart. Let me do my job, Tate. I may not do it perfectly, but I do it well, and justice will be served. I mean the way where you can actually look me in my eyes and thank me for allowing Aliyah to rest. I would reckon for you to take heed and be that monster only inside of your head," I warned before giving the notorious thug a nod.

Instead of replying, he rolled up his window, driving off smoother than four brand new tires. He was definitely working his influence around my damn town, but I was bound to be the first to show him that Athens still belonged to me.

***

Nellie B Projects
10:10 p.m.
Sky Dog

"You crapped out, nigga. Spill some more bread on the floor, or spill yo' broke ass out the front door," I said to Stacy as I broke him for another forty bucks.

The gambling spot out in the Nellie B was lit like a Christmas tree in the summer. Ganja was getting passed around by the bag. A couple of hustlers passed around a little bit of nose candy to loosen the postures around the crib, and all four walls blasted with chatter and clinging forty-ounce beer bottles.

"Broke-ass man, you ain't said nothing. Bet them same weak-ass two dubs again. I'ma have you dropping eighty," he shot back.

"Please! By the time you leave this spot tonight, ya ass might need a ride all the way back to the east side."

The entire house laughed with us as we all enjoyed the usual day around the ghetto. Just as the evening was feeling like nothing could possibly go wrong, my eyes roamed up to Marlon Tate and Titty Head strolling into Stacy's party. I knew that he wasn't invited, so the smell of some fuck shit was quickly starting to surface through the air.

Once the music cut off, Stacy stood to his feet, and all eyes were on two of the men that had a strong hold down on the east side of Athens -truly the whole Classic City.

"Wow, a party throwed in one of my own territories, and nobody, not one single person, thinks to invite me?" He smirked, staring around the room at all the guests.

Stacy could sense the energy and tried to confront them before things got out of hand. "Say M.T., you know I got mad respect for you, homie, but we a bunch of high schoolers. This ain't no place for you guys. You might wanna go hit up the Jaguar or some, all this in here is too young."

"Is that right?" M.T. asked with a raised brow.

Titty's Head gun came out on cue, slapping Stacy clean to the floor. The entire room shouted with an uproar, watching the cold steel put him down.

"Ain't no fucking way," I mumbled to myself, watching the blood slowly drain from his skull.

"See, that's what happen to niggas that speak out of turn!" M.T. was yelling and waving a big-ass pistol.

Everybody was panicking, and I couldn't even protect myself. All my guns were in the car under the seat. These fools was in in this bitch waving weapons like it wasn't a room full of teens, and it made me think of the episode at the school that just recently happened with Jameel.

"I never meant to intrude on you guys' little fuck fest. The Luke can keep playing on when I leave. I just need to know, has anyone seen Li'l Gary running anywhere? We've been on the entire east side swerving around every corner to see him for something very urgent. That name ring any bells?" he asked to no one in particular.

It was like the trail to the Chattahoochee River opened up, exposing Li'l Gary posted on the far couch. A couple of night stalkers were with him. I knew for a fact they couldn't help him. I was just really praying that he didn't kill the guy in my home. M.T. trailed through the room with Titty Head right behind him. He stopped a few feet away from Gary, pointing a sturdy finger.

"I been looking everywhere. It's reached my town that you've been talking to the guys, and I ain't talking about the idiots that standing around you right now. Stand up on your feet, dummy."

I was clenching my jaws so hard that my brain started to shake like a fucking disco club. There was no telling what the little rat had said to the pigs to catch me a bid in the can, or even worse, the feds. I had done dirt around Li'l Gary, and if he was snitching on M.T., it wasn't no question about everyone else who's name could have been involved in anything. Titty Head pointed his gun at him, and his scary ass was on his feet so fast, that his skin nearly sunk under his toes. I can tell by the way he trembled the begging was about to start. I just didn't need any bullshit to occur until he escorted all the interrogation to another location.

"M.T., I swear on my mama's life, man, I ain't said shit to these people. They only held me because they didn't know nothing. I—"

"Nigga always say that shit about they mama, and truly I don't believe anybody that was snatched up by the police and catching shade on the block a few hours later. Move it outside, fuck nigga!" He pointed the gun while pushing him towards the front door.

Li'l Gary stumbled, falling on the floor, and then quickly hopped up. Titty Head was ready to fire off at any minute, so I know that no one was about to buck as we exited the home.

"I had mercy on a lot of you little thugs back then, because I had no pleasure in killing children, but now it seems like you niggas are getting to grown for ya britches. I hate rats, especially one that puts my name in their mouth," M.T. said with malice dripping off his tongue.

The crowd of people was now lined up in front of my apartment, and I could already picture the worst happening in my head in the next few seconds if Li'l Gary said the wrong thing. Titty Head was eyeing him like a vicious wild animal when M.T. smiled, asking him one last question.

"How many licks does it take to get the center of a Tootsie Pop, pussy?" He grinned.

Li'l Gary opened his mouth, but nothing came out. After a few seconds of fumbling with the answer, M.T. spoke for him.

"Only a snitch would be able to tell you!" he spat before nodding his head to Titty Head.

Boc!

Li'l Gary's screams from being shot in the leg were silenced when Titty Head collided his gun across the top of his head, tossing him in the trunk of M.T.'s Mercedes Benz. The sight had everyone stuck, and not one single word was uttered.

"I would advise all of y'all to understand this isn't a talking city. We keep our mouths closed around this way. I would suggest you little kids do the same thing, and it'll all be good. Make sure y'all drink and fuck a little bit for me tonight. We gonna leave y'all to it." M.T. waved his hand, climbing in the passenger seat of his car, as Titty Head jumped behind the wheel and peeled off.

My eyes roamed over to Stacy holding his head standing in the doorway, and I knew shit was about to get far from out of hand. The question now was, who would run their mouth about what just occurred tonight and would Li'l Gary ever be seen again?

Walking back through the small crowd of people in Stacy's crib, I pulled out my cell phone and headed to the bathroom to make a quick call.

Chapter 8
Lexington Apartments
Atlanta, GA
Stanley G

Pulling up inside of the ducked-off set of apartments, me Butta, and Chip Knock stepped out of the car once I parked in front of my main supplier's spot. His name was Rick Willi a known gangster from back in the day that didn't bar none from nobody. He was a thug that ran through the streets of Athens in his younger days, but eventually stepped it up to moving real weight up in Atlanta. Once he got his groove, his name hit the airwaves for being one of the biggest in Georgia to move a key of coke. I had my mans tossing me the major deals, and was eating lovely from the loads he pressed on my table.

As I moved towards his spot, the door opened before I had a chance to knock. A small woman no more than four foot even stuck her head from behind it with a weird mug.

"You're late, Stanley. If you would like to keep remaining apart of anything dealing with this, you'll correct your avenues and buy you a new watch," she informed me before stepping to the side, allowing us to enter.

I didn't know what position she played in his operation, so I chose to keep my mouth closed. I viewed everything in my vision inside of Rick's humble little space. Even though it was a medium-sized living area, it was decked with all the new electronics, fabrics, and features. It was like a mini mansion fully loaded, just on the dangerous side of the suburbs. He was laced with cash, but on a budget, and you know old school niggas worked a certain way when it came down to securing the bag.

Walking into his cocaine-white dining area, I found my mans posted with a cigar in his mouth, reading the AJC newspaper. His Hugo slacks were tailored, and his dress shoes were made by Ferragamo. His slacks were pressed as well. Once he looked up at me his smile turned brighter than a new day.

"Motherfucker, it's about time! How long did it take for you to make it from that baby-ass town of Athens? I was expecting you hours ago." He wrapped me in a brotherly hug.

I made sure to show my best confident face, because Rick was a master for pepping out a problem in the air. It was like the oracle from *The Matrix*. If anything came his way, whether thought or valid information, he picked it apart and split the entire story as if it was a fresh vision to a psychic.

"I'm good, Rick, just a little traffic. I like being late sometimes. It means I get to spend a little longer with you. How's Ann?" I switched the question immediately.

"Take a seat, have a cup of coffee with me. Beth Ann is just fine. She's just on her usual mode of making currency. That woman has a strive harder than the realest trafficker you know."

He walked swiftly over to the counter, grabbing me a glass mug and filling it up with steamed coffee. He took his seat at the table, sliding it over. Quietness grew in the room, and I knew what was coming next. His eyebrows slumped in like an old grump, and his voice was stern when the question left his lips.

"So when were you gonna tell me that you and Marlon T are feuding all over Classic City? It's like the news reporters are calling my line themselves."

I took a sip of my coffee, pondering on how I would come. Rick wasn't stupid, but he also wasn't with the negativity. He would end business quick with a hot-tempered clientele, and there was no room for me to lose out on any money at the moment in Athens. Instead of containing the secret, I kept it straight G.

"Look, Rick, you've been dealing with me since I was eighteen, big homie. I've never landed trouble on your doorstep. I've dealt with business accordingly, and it's never been any slips from me. I'm clean with what I do, and I'm gonna continue to do it with you professionally as I've always done. The question about Marlon… He's grown and trying to overstep boundaries as if I'm a child. Friend or no friend, I'm staying in my lane, so I won't hesitate to kill him. He's on a rampage about something that hasn't been brought to my attention yet, so unfortunately, I'm at war with a nutcase without a proper excuse to even give you. I'm lost, Rick," I explained before leaning back in my seat.

He crossed his arms with a displeased expression. I can see that he was feeling some type of way, but knew that he cared for the pure heart, and I just happened to be that pure-hearted nigga.

"Stanley, you're at the top of your game with a lead that most people couldn't touch. You're smart, and I don't mean smart that eventually falls for being too damn good. I mean smart ones that never get caught and retire with everything, and more. Still with their lives and family. I even think you're so smart that I can bet you even know when to play your cards and fold. M.T. is not the avenue you need to embark on right now if you have thoughts of making any of that shit I just explained reality, son."

"What do you mean?"

"I mean that boy is dangerous, just as much as you. So wipe the arrogance. Stay clear from him, even if it means to turn the other way. I've seen him get nasty, and I'm not trying to see a clash between the two kings of Athens. We're here to make money, so fuck your feelings, because he's gonna get the same message once his voice picks up through my line. My ears are always open, Stanley. If you have a problem from now on, just run it by me or find another plug." He shrugged as if he were giving me that option to choose from at that exact second.

I knew that M.T. was a dog in the turf, but I was just as much of a pit as he was, and I was known for biting first. Hiding my anger with a mask. I smiled and agreed with sincerity. "Rick, my respect for you goes above the average man. Most nigga's words can get flushed down the toilet when it comes to telling me to stand down about my life, my business, my honor. Your words are more because they stick to me like a father. So whatever you say is bond. You have my word." I gazed him square in the eyes.

His leg shook with a straight Marine Corp posture. No blinking, stiff-chested, and blank-faced. "That's the reason you will be a king in this world. Hold on to that. You're gonna leave this world a legend." His smile eventually rose back, and he stood to his feet. "Come on, take a walk with me." He waved me his hand towards his back patio door.

Motioning for my guards to remain positioned, I followed Rick outside to the porch. The entire space was filled with fishing equipment, marble tiles, and red bricks. At least half the ground was covered with the working material. It was like Rick was getting ready to build a driveway for his apartment.

"Have you ever dug a hole before, Stanley?" he asked me, looking around at all the materials.

"Nah, unfortunately, I don't do digging."

"If any bull presents itself, you need one for all the bodies around you. If your name gets mixed in anything, you kill all of your small crew members and start fresh. I'm not taking chances on anyone setting you up, let alone building a case against us when you catch the right charge. Understood?" he asked, puffing on his cigar heavily.

The statement made my heart shift a bit, but I knew that he just meant business. "I understand clearly."

"Good." He smirked, walking a few feet over to a silver barbeque grill, opening the top. He removed a duffle and tossed it to me. Catching it, I tossed it around my back with a nod.

"That's fourteen. The extra two are on the house for your good hospitality. Now go and have you some fun tonight. Go on a date or something. You can break your supply down tomorrow. Same time. Two weeks," he said before starting to rearrange a few things in his way.

Exiting off his back porch, I took the long way around the building to get back to the car. Rick never allowed entrance back in the crib once you've left and received anything from his possession. My two soldiers had already been escorted back to the car by the assistant in Rick's spot. No one knew that simple people that seemed normal around Rick were wolves in sheep's clothing. I knew each murderer bodyguard he kept close, and skinny lady Mia was the nightmare you would never see gun you down before you knew that you were dead.

I made it back to the front parking lot. Chip Knock and Butta were posted by the car, looking clueless. I climbed in the back seat, stuffing the bag under the seat. Once they closed the doors, pulling away from our destination, Chip Knock looked at me through the rearview mirror from the driver's seat.

"So I mean, did the nigga stitch your mouth up or what, big bro? Is the business good? What happened?" he asked.

"We good. I just can't afford no more incidents. We about to eat. That's all you need to know."

"That's what I'm talking about," Butta butted in.

"That's all good too, but hey, I'm ya li'l brother. I gotta know what's going when I'm sliding with you. We all trust each other. I mean, we gotta make the money together. Just know it's to make sure shit smooth when my mouth opens up, my nigga, period." He slid into the gas station Citgo beside the apartments.

"As I said, you my mans, so stop asking, 'cause I'll never repeat shit, Chip. That's to keep myself safe, and also you. We need to keep out workers grinding hard, but be on the lookout for that fool M.T. I want everyone to stand down, let him be, but if he pushes down on any oppression shit, kill him quietly and bring me the body. I'll get rid of it myself."

He never replied, but the head nod and change of face let me knew that he got the picture.

I was on my way to being the golden boy from Classic City, and I wasn't gonna let nothing block that, no matter what the cost.

* * *

Six hours later
Westside of Athens
Toot

Taking the last bite of my sausage biscuit, I swallowed the orange juice from my glass and tossed it into the sink. I had to meet with M.T. within the next hour to go ahead and handle my recent problems with Stanley. The way my mind saw it, if I couldn't beat you, then I would feed you to the next nigga that could. No nigga around our way could pass up the info on all your stash houses and family addresses. It was more than ten ways to skin a cat, and I was about to show this tough man who was leading the race.

Tucking my .380 in my back, I headed for the door. When I opened it up, a black Glock 40 pressed against the center of my forehead, caused me to shudder. I was pushed back in the house, and the two men that fell in behind me quickly slammed the door with eyes scanning the house like the SWAT team. It was Pooleg and Freaky. I knew at that moment that Stanley had obviously taken a step before I could even lift my leg.

"You know what this is about, correct?" Pooleg asked in a low tone.

My lips shivered so fast that I couldn't physically reply, but I shook my head.

"Is anybody else in this bitch?" Freaky took a few steps, looking around.

I shook my head again. I knew that I wasn't being robbed because the two fools in front of me weren't good at anything but taking souls, but I wondered what was the pause if they strictly came for me. My li'l shorty was asleep in the bedroom two doors down, so I didn't want to panic them if I still had a chance.

"Toot, where's the money you owe Stanley? I'm gonna give you one chance to be real so we can get what we need and be on our way. If you lie, I can't say that we just gonna push on so easy, bruh-bruh?

"The money is still short ten G's, Pooleg. Me and Stanley just recently talked. It's no way he not trusting me to handle my end. I just needed a few more days, baby. Y'all niggas has got to be crazy!" I spat with sweat starting to form on my head.

"I said where is it?" he asked again, this time racking the gun back.

"Under that blue nightstand over by the wall. The bottom of it pulls out to a small stash spot. Don't pop me!"

I watched Pooleg destroy the stand within seconds and the twenty grand that's was stashed slapped against the ground before he gently picked it all up with a grin. He nodded at Freaky, who still had me at gunpoint. His pupils dilated, like a Roxy prescription pill just hit his system, as he opened his mouth.

"You cooperating today just helped you out, Toot. The debt for the remaking ten grand is clear, and you did a good deed by telling the truth. You just have to get God to accept it, baby boy."

"Wait, I thought you was gon' honor me being gutta. My whole girl, in the room, young gun. Don't do me like this. Spare me. My baby is gonna have to see me dead, killer. You don't want that shit on this bitch's conscience. Please?" I begged.

"I thought you said no one else was here?" Pooleg stared at me with venom in his expression.

Before I could say anything else, he was searching rooms one by one. As he reached the room where my woman slept, the sound of two slugs sounded off, forcing me to scream.

"Noooooo!" I jumped towards Freaky's gun, and all I remember was hearing the gun sound off and a bright light.

Chapter 9
Broad Acer Apartments
7:30 p.m.
Elmadi

After alerting everybody on my snatch and grab team about our meeting earlier, I had finally arrived to discuss our next mission. My mind was already on the next level to make sure any expenses Andre's family needed, they would have, but I was also thinking for the real score. If I wanted to do what I needed, I was gonna have to take what I wanted, and I was ready to build my own wealth at the same time. The next plan on my list wasn't easy as grabbing a pair of jeans from a store rack. It was breaking glass and see who could snatch the most priceless jewelry without getting nabbed. I had recently done my homework on the location, and if I calculated shit right, we could hit for fifty thousand dollars with the safe and jewels alone. We were gonna need a five-man team, and I had just the men to pull it off with me.

After tapping two times on the apartment door, it was opened by my cousin Vida, and I walked in. My crew was already present: Stacy, Sky Dog, and BoRat. The new member was a young hothead from the east side, Li'l Jermaine, Chip knock's first cousin. He was a go-getter, and truly the only kid that could rock with a sneaky crew like mines. I liked that.

Once I made sure the door was locked, I took off my jacket and sat at the table with the rest of the fellas.

"I'm glad all y'all boys made it. It lets me know that it ain't no room for playing, and y'all wanna get some money. So I'll go ahead and break it down like this. This snatch and grab ain't the usual, so I feel you if any one of y'all wanna back down at any time, besides when we get in front of this bitch. It's a jewelry store over on the east side in a busy plaza. I'm talking about nine to ten grand apiece in cash if we in there for thirty seconds tops. Not including diamonds. I, for one, am tired of these few grand that flies away after we look out for our girls and mamas. The way I see it, there's a few of these around the outskirts of Georgia, and we will have enough to swap it up after a three-month vacation." I gave it to them straight.

They all sat quiet, and I noticed the discomfort in Stacy's eyes when jewelry store was mentioned. He was definitely shook. BoRat, Vida, and Sky Dog damn near sang in unison for agreement, so the hard part was over.

I clasped my hands in good graces and got up to pour me a cup of vodka. I walked around pondering on the entire plot .It was foolproof, and I knew after my first strike I was adding ten grand towards whoever's head that took Andre's life.

"We 'bout to get this bread, but it's time to turn it up a notch, y'all, just smartly and unnoticeably. We gotta move smooth like we dead around here. I know the perfect way."

"Hold on, fool, what you mean move like we dead? You mean like Chucky with the spirit doll shit, right? 'Cause no one never saw that li'l mu'fucka!" BoRat laughed.

I couldn't do nothing but shake my head at his slow ass. I just knew what his muscle was worth. "No, jackrabbit, I mean like a CIA agent, like a spy. Give me one month of staying off the scene, and I can probably bet my life that we can be counting up a hundred grand in a new spot. That's only if we stick with my plan without showing our faces period, unless necessary." I broke it down smoothly as possible.

"Man, that's understood. When is this gonna lift up? 'Cause I don't like talking." Vida smirked calmly.

I had to think and make sure I wasn't rushing the move, but my mind was made up. "We hit it next Saturday. Right before closing time." I leaned back against the wall, resting my eyes.

Once we all came to the final conclusion, we passed a few blunts around and headed out the door to make it back for our normal schedule. The moment we hit the parking lot, dispersing to our separate cars, four unmarked silver Tahoes pulled up, speeding, and stopped in front of us all. A swarm of armed officers exited the vehicles, guns up, and running wasn't even in the option.

"Get on your fucking knees and cross your hands now. All of you!!" an officer screamed, pointing his AR-15 with precision.

"Shit, man!" Sky Dog cursed.

We all gave each other another look before following orders. Within a few seconds, we were all restrained in cuffs, and I watched a suited man step through the crowd with a yellow folder in hand.

"Elmadi Glade. You and your little butt buddies here are wanted for questioning." He smiled with sarcasm.

"Questioning? You can just ask us did we gangbang ya wife right here? All this shit shouldn't be necessary." I shrugged my shoulders.

"Right." He nodded with a smile. "We need to see how you feel when I pin Andre's body on you, and also that mall y'all dumb asses just damaged a few days back. Tell me how it sounds when we get there." He waved his hand towards the officers behind us.

We were all quickly thrown in the back of a separate truck besides me and Stacy. From the look of how hard the cops tuned in to our every move, I knew we had a long night ahead of us.

*   *   *

Athens Police Precinct.
Detective L. Foster

Even after sitting in the precinct with these little idiots for the last four hours, I had gotten not one piece of evidence to throw any one of them behind walls until a court date was appointed. I used all the information that the informant Li'l Gary gave me about the individuals, but since then, I couldn't get an answer from the cell line he gave me, nor did he make the daily visit that he was obligated to in exchange for his freedom. One of the little pricks had already got granted a phone call, so I knew one parent and lawyer was on the way. The others weren't far behind. None of these guys was over the age of twenty, so it told me something might occur behind the faulty arrest if I couldn't get a snake to slide.

I headed in the room with the kid Elmadi. He locked eyes with me as I strolled calmly over to the table, taking a seat.

"So do you think we need to talk now? It's hard to tell you this, but these charges will be stuck on you whether in court or tonight before your people can walk inside this building. I know things that I shouldn't, Glade. Like your antics and sneaky moves for snatching up merchandise that isn't paid for. I also see you have some influence. It's just not gonna work in here, or with me. What if it I tell you, if you help me out, I can make sure the courts never bother you? You won't even receive a court document in your mailbox, like this will all be a mistake on the department's behalf? I just need to know who's all moving with you inside those malls, and all the info you have on your best friend being shot in the head," I offered with empathy.

He still remained quiet with his fingers intertwined. I couldn't find any fear on his aura, so I continued to stare him down, burning my anger through his small-ass skull. "I can tell you this, Glade. This game of chess that's being played, I will win, and anyone behind this conspiracy with you will get so much time, they're gonna have a jacuzzi personally built for you lip soft tissue punks. We have a witness screaming about you knowing the reason your friend was murdered. I sure hope like hell it isn't true, 'cause if so, Li'l Gary will be the reason you catch 20 plus four hundred years, dumbass." I laughed with a winning grin.

The sound of Li'l Gary's name rattled something, because his body locked up like a cat being thrown in a tub. He tried to catch himself, but I caught his ass a little faster.

"Does that name ring any bells, fool? You have a case that's about to be built against you like the Taliban. Do you have anything to say for your own defense?" I waited to see if he would speak.

Lowering his gaze, he exhaled heavily, with a sigh behind it by the second.

"The only thing I can tell you is that the gangbang with your lady didn't take all those men. She wanted extra by choice. Plus, I saved a bunch of money on my car insurance by switching to the General with Shaq." He flicked me off.

Just as I jumped across the counter to punch out a permanent tooth, my superior and a scrawny, black lawyer entered the room, looking like his suit belonged on Nutty Professor. He had a pair of thick glasses over his eyes. Judging from my captain's face, this was a guy that wasn't too nice. Pulling a few pieces of paper from his manila envelope, he placed them on the desk.

"You've violated my client's rights by not reading him his Miranda rights, and you kept questioning him after I had been contacted without me present, assaults with your hands, and reverse psychology to tempt these young men out of something you want to hear, and I'm quite sure I have another list of charges that can get you thrown into a prison cell directly besides him, if you cheat to convict him. All five of the kids' bonds have been paid, signed by a magistrate judge, and they are requested for immediate release until we meet in court. Elmadi, stand up please," he ordered the teen as if he was the new authority.

I balled up my fist, letting my anger slip. "Now just wait one damn minute. There are a bunch of criminals in this building and you sound like someone that like helping them roam our streets. It smells like a little dirty shit in the air the way you're talking, big shot!" I pointed at him with aggression.

He crossed his hands before giving me his arrogant reply. "Sir, if you don't know, I'm one of the best lawyers in Athens, let alone the state of Georgia. It sounds like you're recommending your background checks to be monitored, as you do this easy conniving job you do so well. I'll be sure to alert my private investigator to track every step you take. Elmadi, we can leave now." He opened the door, waiting for him to follow.

The young prick stood up, walking over to the captain, holding the cuffs out in the air. When he removed them, he turned around, making a motion for someone sucking his dick, and that solidified me fucking up his entire life, and it was a promise I was willing to lose it all for.

"I warned you not to make any false move to have the other side on our asses. It seems like you just can't take orders like good duty cops are used to, Foster. You're suspended for a week with pay, and you are not allowed to work on investigations of any sort. Put your gun in storage and clock out," the captain spat with malice before slamming the interrogation room door, leaving me to myself.

I drove my balled fist into the table before kicking a chair forcefully towards the wall watching it break in two. The sight of every teen I arrested walking out of that door boiled my skin like a hot link, and I fought myself not to put one of them to sleep in front of the entire precinct. Before the last individual walked out of the front entrance, his head turned back, catching sight of my face. He nodded, placing a finger to his lips, and my upside-down frown started to flip. If I was a madman, I would say that I had me a dirty friend that was ready to stop being shined on, one that wouldn't mind giving me a form of peace, for a root of nastiness that could never be overruled. Money.

Chapter 10
Wanda's Spot
Rockspring Apartments
Elmadi

After gaining my freedom back out of the nasty precinct office, it forced me to head in for the remainder of the night. I realized that I had nothing better to do, with Monica stuck in her attitude at her mama's. The boys were ducked off and my first, Kim, was a distance away from me. I called someone who showed sincere love, no matter what time of the day, year, or moment.

Wanda had allowed me to make my way over, and even fixed a little dinner to bite on as we sat back and vibed about everything in the brain. I was close to her because of the bond, but also the similarities in us both. We were like two geniuses that could only turn each other's knobs. The friendship is what always held that firmly in place.

"So what are you gonna do with the rest of your life after you graduate officially, Elmadi? I mean, graduation is over, but we pick up our real diplomas and scholarship resumés next week. What are your plans after that?"

I had to sit back and think because unlike most, I actually graduated from school and had good enough credits to enter some of the best universities. My mind was on money, and at the same time Andre. So much clutter was in my way that school wasn't nowhere in my mental at the moment.

"I don't know, Wanda. I'm not really worried about the college life right now. I still got Andre's mama to help out with the bill from his burial. I got a mama, a child on the way, and silly-ass friends to help guide. Too much pressure to go anywhere. Really a risk," I replied truthfully.

She sat up on my bed and gave me that look as if she wanted to shoot a slap my way. Her caramel skin was glowing like the lightbulb in the ceiling, and her hazel eyes danced and sparkled with curiosity.

"That was probably the stupidest shit I've ever heard you say the entire time we've known each other. It's always been your dream for college and psychology. Why the sudden change now?"

To be honest, I knew that I had a lot of pressure on me, and it was gonna be hard for her to understand what responsibility I couldn't just walk away from. "I gotta lotta shit that's on my slab, Wanda. I just can't abandon it for some college that's claiming they want the best for me. It's a small chance that those people expect my bright side wholeheartedly and I'm damn sure about family being more of a priority as of right now. Ever since Andre was murdered, that dream kind of died with my mans. He had high hopes for me doing all that. Them days changed."

"I knew I needed more ambition when it came to my thinking, but my heart was set on where it was at when I said I wanted to be a doctor, Elmadi. We made those dreams together as children. Andre's ambition was to be the man. No one cared about what he did in the streets, nor the ones you were with. They only cared for the things you and Andre could do for them, the kind of things that could benefit them with you being around or not. Do you get that at all?" She touched my head repeatedly with her index finger.

"Yeah, I do. I ain't said I don't get it at all. I said it's not my main focus, Wanda, calm down."

"You're saying calm down, but I'm watching you switch gears like nothing ever mattered, Elmadi. Okay, let's say you have a right to be mad. How would you handle the killing if you did happen to find out who did it to Andre? Regardless of how many bullets you shoot or bodies you drop, he still will be in the same spot that he was in before you started. None of that can bring him back. How do you think he would feel looking down on you knowing that you spent life in prison, or worse, death because of his loss?"

I truly couldn't come up with anything to say even though my heart wanted to keep going against what she felt. There was nothing like losing a close friend that nearly gave you half of everything coming up. It was the only way I maintained at my lowest, or even when I had my best times. He was the helping hand that broke even to make it possible. So if his repayment caused a group of motherfuckers to go, then it was stamped.

"Why is it that I can find the right and loveable answers from no one else but you?": I gave her a light peck on the cheek before cuddling back close to her.

We were indeed best friend, ones that would never stop for anyone. I listened closely to every word she voiced, and needed all the advice she wanted to offer. It wasn't the normal when you had a Queen that would cross right knowledge through to a person while they experienced whatever trial God decides to take them within. She was my peace to the calming storm inside me

"Because, big head, I'm the best with love and realness. You ain't heard? Wendy Williams ain't got smack on me. You just have to make sure you smile more than frown, and if you can't, then you have to let the ones around you go that's causing it to happen, E," She said softly

"You're right. That's one thing I can say, Wanda."

"And if they can't change it, they shouldn't even come around you. Period. Now out of all people, I never thought anyone could control your dark-ass emotions. You're like

Casanova himself." She walked over to the small fridge against my wall to grab an orange juice.

My mind bounded back to the lick I had struck hard at Georgia Square mall, I dug into my pockets and peeled off six hundred dollar bills, closing my distance with Wanda. I put them in her palm. "Take this, and do something nice for yourself. Rent, clothes, whatever you choose." I grinned with that smile that always made her blush.

Wanda was never the type to complain. She always just rocked with the flow. I tried to speak my mind on something else, but she covered my mouth before I could. Unzipping my pants and undoing my belt with her loose hand, she killed the lights and led me to the bed

"Now you know I hate when you give me money. Where did you get it anyway?" she asked with her lips nearly touching mines in the dark.

"Doesn't matter, because it's yours now. Stop sitting around needing if you know I got. I can help you more than just when a bed's around."

Climbing on top of me, she smacked her lips. "Nigga, you wish! Your middle name is Bed. You must forgot I been knowing you, fool!" She laughed, grabbing the sheet, pulling it over us

* * *

After opening my eyes about an hour later, I realized me and Wanda had passed out. It was going on five in the morning, and I knew that I had a ton of shit to do today besides play house. Waking her gently, I rubbed the small of her back.

"You mind if the guys come through here later on for our next meeting?

She tooted up her nose, showing her answer without saying it. "I'm not sure. I don't wanna rack my brain about if these niggas will rob me blind when I'm not looking. Would I have to attend to all these knuckleheads?" she snapped like I was making her think too hard.

Quickly sliding on a pair of pants, I headed for the living room. I knew for a fact that I couldn't sit down with anyone else about my next move. Sky Dog and Vida was really the only two that I could trust, BoRat too, but my head started to tell me differently about Stacy, something I just hadn't figured out yet.

Stepping inside my family room, I froze in horror at M.T. posted up on her couch. Titty Head was posted by the front door. Silence filled the air around them. Wanda's mother was passing M.T. a steaming cup of tea and didn't know that she was under the wing of a true demon.

"How did he get in here?" I said with seriousness lacing my vocals.

She gave me a crazed look before turning back to him. I watched him glance at me and his face formed a true Athens slum mug. His coffee mug fell to the floor, and the gun Titty Head cuffed behind his back was being revealed. Wanda's mama tried to run, but he caught her by the hair before she could get any distance from him.

"Where you going, bitch? I guess my woman is a free pick for letting niggas in to do what they please huh?"

My feet moved to rush at her aid, but Titty Head's .357 slowed me down. "Freeze yo' ass, boy! Before you can't remember what happened tomorrow."

"Man, come on, M.T., that's my step mama," I begged.

I had never stepped into the maniac's lane, so I was clueless on what he was doing at Wanda's home. He was a drug dealer that only dealt with bosses, so to see him in

Rocksprings at five in the morning had me truly stuck. I held my hands up, trying to ease his anger and also to prevent Mama Kee from being shot. My heart felt like it was about to go out at any second until Wanda's voice caught me off guard.

"Nigga, you really got some nerve! After all I have on my board, you pull over here to do something like this? Let my mama go or I'm calling the police!" She held a chrome .38 snub nose. It only held five shots, but the bullets were big enough to knock a hole into a Dodge Ram truck with ease.

His anger simmered when he looked at her. Titty Head clutched on his gun, but he tapped his shoulder as if he was giving him the sign to calm down. Pushing her mother towards her, he folded his arms.

"It's crazy that my woman has a whole high school nigga in here, not to mention he's friends with the dead man that stole the rims from my Cadillac. I paid real numbers for those, numbers that could easily make the right man find your home and stay over for dinner." He glared at me up and down.

"Fuck that! I'm not your woman anymore, Marlon, and I'm not gonna ask you twice about leaving my home." Wanda clutched the gun tighter.

M.T. blew a kiss before asking me a question. "How about you can tell me where I can find my boy so I can be on about my way? Just give me a clue, and I'm sure the rest will find me."

I didn't want to say anything that was gonna lead to somebody dying, but I had no choice but to let Jameel handle his own since he was man enough to risk all of us in his nonsense. "He's in a house close to Alps Road. That's all I know." I stood firm on my lie.

M.T. rotated his head between me and Wanda a few times before exiting the front door.

I helped her mama up once the door closed, but I couldn't help to stare at Wanda. It was more going on than I knew, and before it could even be asked, she spilled it to me.

"We used to date each other, E. I've been broken up with him for six months now, but he does psychotic shit like this. I'm sorry I never warned you about it earlier, but I promise you I have no ties or dealings with him. He just won't leave me alone," she expressed with exhaustion.

Giving her a solid hug and kiss, I lifted her chin. "Don't sweat it. You've had my back through thick and thin, so you know I'm here in return. I'm gonna stay away for a few weeks, but I will be watching this crib. I need to get something handled, and I don't need you showing any signs. Just continue to be cool, and if anybody asks have you seen me, lie," I said, heading for the door.

Chapter 11
Jameel

It had been weeks since I went to school or even stepped foot out of my house. I was laying low after the scene in my high school parking lot. I wasn't trying to hide from my problem, but I damn sure wasn't about to face 'em either. All types of weird-ass calls, even messages, had been received at my house within the last few days, and I just happened to be blessed to answer every time before my mother. I didn't want her to deal with my issues, especially when it came to her safety.

Walking out of my bedroom, I headed for the kitchen. I shitted out my heart when I noticed M.T. sitting next to my mother on our sofa. The same nigga that was present at the school with him last time was grinning ear to ear as he rubbed on my mother's thigh.

"Well, well, well, if it ain't the man I needed to see. Jameel, right?" M.T. started to play with my mother's hair.

She was so terrified that I could see the silent tears drop from her face. I couldn't leave my mama out there for free bargain. I stumbled over my words, not knowing exactly how to reply. I just didn't want to dig my mama a deeper hole, so I gave him the scoop.

"Yeah, I'm Jameel, M.T., and I already know that you're here about your rims. I can tell you exactly who put me up to doing this, because I would have never touched a car that belongs to you if I was aware. This obviously was a set-up that's falling back on me!" I shouted to see if I had the opportunity for my mama to get up and come to me.

"So who helped you? I would suggest you give me all names if you even think they have a part in with this?"

I didn't want to cross anyone, but it was a matter of life and death.

“Man it was E’s boy, man. The booster who go to my school. He didn’t know anything about it, but his li’l workers is the one that told me the Cadillac was a retired Marine’s, so I took the chance to get some quick money. It was Sky Dog and Stacy. That’s the only thing I can tell you, M.T., I swear, but please, man, that’s my mother. Don’t cause no harm to her for me. You can have me,” I pleaded.

“You stole a pair of eight thousand dollar rims, and that has to be shown some attention. You ran from me when I showed up to the school, and that’s where you made your first and last mistake. I would rather you rob me before pulling a coward-ass low stunt. Don’t you know that I run this city?”

A moment of silence filled the room, and I watched M.T. deliver my mama a hard right punch to the face, catching her in his arms before she could hit the floor.

“Motherfuckerrrr!” I raged, watching my mom go unconscious.

Titty Head collided his gun directly across my nose, shattering it on impact.

“Fuckkkk!”

I fell to my knees, cuffing the running blood that was pouring from my shit. The ringing in my ears finally stopped. That’s when I noticed M.T. take a few steps over, staring down at me like dying prey in the jungle. My sight focused in on him, and his face became clear through all the dizziness.

“You know you fucked now, right? And I ain’t talking ’bout *Menace to Society*. In this hood, I’m like God, boy. It ain’t no way around me. Now after you tell me where my rims are, I wanna know any name that could have some to do with my little cousin Aliyah dying at that graduation party. Something gotta give, Jameel.”

"I already told everybody that I don't know 'bout that. You can't force me to lie to you about something I don't know." I tried to explain my end.

M.T. raised his hand to his mouth for me to stop talking, and for some reason, I felt that I wasn't gonna make it out of this with my life. The sight of my mother laying on the floor caused me to mumble a silent prayer for some relief, but the devil was present and making sure that he was known to destroy whatever he could.

"Well, I guess you can try again once more after you awake from the light slumber."

"Wait!" I raised my hand, trying to plea with the unmerciful killer above me.

Halfway through my sentence, Titty Head's foot raised above my head. Once I felt the vicious kick that was delivered to my face, the entire room faded black.

* * *

Stanley G

Sitting in the living room of my new suppliers and clientele, I waited patiently for him to reach me so this deal for the new batch of heroin could drop head first on the streets of Athens. I had been on three different trips in the last two days to find the best quality, not to mention the sweetest prices. Even though I was in business with Rick, my hustling mentality edged me on to not settle for all my eggs in his basket, so I expanded the resources in case shit ever flew south. Athens was a few days short behind the fast-moving town of Atlanta, and our numbers were completely different. After maximizing the capital of Georgia, I brought it back to my block and sparked a new era.

Lexx, my plug, walked into his living room just as my shining moments faded to the back of my membrane. He was sporting a Calvin Klein sweat suit and a pair of Tommy Hilfiger slippers. Gold was drizzled on his neck and wrist, and my eyes saluted the Plain Jane Rolex that didn't look as if it cost under twenty grand.

"Stanleyyy, the best gangster I know in the state of America. How has life been treating you, bad man? Tell me something good." He sat down at the coffee table as if he was allergic to getting dirty.

"I'm good, Lexx, business is great. Athens is still my throne, and I'm having all that a man could possibly ask for in his land. This was my dream. It's just other people drifting in it."

Lexx smiled, shaking his head. "You don't have to explain the extra to me, man. I'm we'll alert of what you do and how you do. I have five keys for you, and this isn't the joke. It's raw, so be careful to how you serve the fiends. You might have a temple of deceased corpses, and that's like a million years bad luck. Besides work, how are you feeling mentally, kiddo?" He titled his head, trying to look me in the face.

"I feel like I have the greatest mentality that I could ever reach. Just when I meet a new limit, I see that it can reach further. This was my game built with the specifics to coach me alone. I can never be out of my safe space." I shrugged my shoulders with no care.

The middle-aged man got up, grabbing my product from off his office desk in far corner. My henchman also placed a bag of bills in his hand for return. He huffed with a finger pointing at me so I didn't even force a word from my lips.

"I believe in you, probably more than you believe in yourself. You have a strong persona about you, Stanley, and that's what you should always keep concealed for direct moments when needed. Some people fear uniqueness; others tend to grow a bad hatred for it. The longer you remain humble and unreadable, the more you make an avenue to rise, my friend. Slow down and know when enough is enough. Those are the real gangsters. Trust me on that." He held out his hand

Shaking it firmly, I placed a hand on his shoulder. "Hiding something is a trait that I don't have, Lexx, so if I have to die for this talented man to be shown forever, then so be it. Let the light keep shining on." I laughed before turning on my heels to leave.

I was dressed down in all hood gear to blend in with a little of the Atlanta areas. Within another year or so, I was gonna count down how long it would take me to run the entire thing. I t was the next stop on my list after I handled my issues in Athens and stamp my name on every curve.

Chapter 12
Bishop Park
Seven days later
Elmadi

The last few days had felt so surreal with all the recent chaos around me that I literally felt like the world was colliding down on my head. I was aware that Monica was pregnant and getting more annoying by the minute. Even though she was ready to have child, I didn't see things working eye to eye with us being so young and curious about the shit we still wanted to do in life.

It was July the Fourth, and after meeting up with Wanda and my nigga BoRat at Bishop Park, we sat back to kick it and get a good day plotting and thinking. Half of Athens was out today and families were all around tossing fresh meat on the grill. Music was live with plenty of fellas and women engaged in their own likes and festivities. It was cooler than cool.

"So you mean to tell me they found Jameel's mama in the house, beat all up, and nobody has seen him? He's really nowhere to be found?" BoRat asked me twice like I was lying.

"Yeah, pretty much. I still can't get over that shit. It's too much funny business going on, but it ain't nobody answering for it. You ain't notice all our friends and people close to us have been getting attacked like crazy?"

He paused, thinking for himself, and I knew the answer he deciphered was going to be the same as mines, but BoRat had to be BoRat. "Uh, yeah, but I thought that's what happened to folks that did dumb shit. What do you expect? This ain't Sunnyville, E, and Superman doesn't swoop in and save people for every crime committed. We in the ghetto, Elmadi."

I truly had to sit back and ponder on that shit, because he partially made sense about pulling stupid shit in one of the most dangerous neighborhoods in Georgia. The reality part of it was real simple. You will always receive the same cards you've dealt out, so it was wise to learn how to work them effectively.

My attention was taken when I noticed three all-white Yukon trucks pull quickly upon inside of the park, but only one was quaking a rap song from the lyricist Scarface. They all stopped in unison. I saw M.T. step out of one of the driver's seats along with a gang of his shooters. My eyes jolted back over to Stanley Gerald and his entourage living it up for the Fourth without a worry in the world. My heart damn near skipped a beat witnessing these two nutcases in the same vicinity. It was only one way things were going when two dons like him and Stanley met in the field. That was either a handshake, or guns drawing.

"Now this isn't the average TV show a nigga see every day. What are the odds both of these boys hitting up Bishop Park on the Fourth?" I tapped BoRat's shoulder to get his attention.

Of course he smiled, probably anticipating the worst to occur on the peaceful day, but something told me nothing was gonna be able to stop the two from crashing, if the little word of mouth about their beef was actually true.

"Now this ain't nothing I wanna see flip out of control, but I'll be damned if I don't get front row seats to this. Let's get a li'l closer." He moved quickly heading towards the center of the park where most of the crowded civilians stood.

"BoRat, this has nothing to do with us, slow down!" I tried to force him to stay back.

His feet were moving faster than usual, and even though I didn't want to be on the scene, I found myself trailing right behind this clown. By the time we closed the gap, getting near the group of men, I watched Stanley lock vision with M.T. His posture switched from humble to rage, and he wasted no time heading straight for him. I cleared the distance between me and BoRat. We stopped in our tracks just as M.T. and Stanley met face to face. We were probably no more than thirty feet away from them, but the conversation made it seem as if they were inches away from our ears.

"I guess it's not so much of a pleasure, but hey, I recognize the time for a sit down. I'm hoping that's the only reason you're approaching me and my team." Stanley flashed M.T. a fearless expression.

"Nah, nigga, it's no pleasure at all. I guess God made it my business to step foot on this park soil today. Out of all the fuckery that's taken place, I would've thought you'd be on the next flight out of the country before you ended up running back into me. Blood has been shed, and if I'm not getting any answers, we might have a problem!" M.T.'s chest heaved with aggression.

The group of both men team stood off, daring the opposite side to make the wrong move. The innocent bystanders began to spread out. It was known who laid the street laws down in Athens, so to see them in each other's presence stopped traffic. I thought Stanley was gonna reply with a smooth line, but instead, he replied with a right hook to M.T.'s jaw. The reverse strike was quicker, with M.T. retaliating with a three-piece that slight stumbled Stanley.

The park started to become rowdy, and you could see that both men's shooters wanted to join in with the bullshit. Instead they all kept it playa and allowed the fade to go down.

Both men were fighting like dogs, but M.T. was brawling like a UFC heavyweight championship on the line. I couldn't believe what my eyes were witnessing, but I knew for a fact that someone was bound to die after all was said and done.

"Where the hell a recorder at when you need one? This shit epic. Two kingpins fighting in the middle of a hot-ass park in Athens on a Friday night. These niggas gotta want to go to jail." BoRat jumped around with excitement.

"Nigga, we need to be getting the fuck outta here before some body start shooting, fool. I got a .38 with six bullets, and I need them to make sure I get all the way back to Rolling Ridge within six minutes.

I was trying my best to lure this fool away from all the nonsense, but the thrill of two killers battling to the death amused this dumb-ass boy. In the midst of me trying to break free from the crowd, I watched M.T. jump off his feet, shooting a hard right kick. Stanley threw up his arm to defend it, but wound up short.

"Shittt!" Stanley crumbled to ground, clutching his arm in severe pain. I could see from the small distance that his shit was broken by the way it dangled.

M.T. was standing back, breathing like Tarzan after wrestling with a six hundred pound gorilla. He broke off with his team hastily back to their vehicles that waited a distance away

"You dead, nigga. That's word to Classic City and my mama!" Stanley barked as he climbed back to his feet.

The Coogi sweater that he wore was drenched in red mud and green grass streaks. His muscles flared up like he was Hulk Hogan, and I was pretty positive that Death was the only agenda on his mind.

"I want blood, and I want all of it. It's only fucking blood from this point on!" Stanley yelled, looking at all his men.

The park was nearly clear, and thirty-three seconds later, my hypothesis proved to be right because the Athens PD were filling up the side entrance by the load. I watched Stanley's crew move closer to a crowd to blend in for a smooth getaway. Niggas was tossing dope sacks and pistols left and right and the cool vibe that was just plastered in the air quickly drowned in the wind.

“Okay, now I think it’s time to get the fuck on.” BoRat busted a U-turn, grabbing me by the shoulder like I did him earlier.

“If you ain’t trying to become a bird eye, you better skate!”

“What?”

I didn’t know what the hell he was talking about, but I had just turned seventeen, which meant straight to the big house, prison block. That shit was out of the question, so I just ran right along besides his crazy ass. The one thing that scanned back through my mind was the look M.T. gave me before he jumped back into his truck. It was a look that said I needed to watch my back!

* * *

Rico Curry

"Damn it!"

I was cursing myself in a fit, thinking hard as I drove down the streets of Athens. These niggas were close to fighting and causing deadly harm with all these Bruce Lee-ass altercations I was hearing about. I didn’t get the full scoop on what was the reason, but I damn sho’ didn’t need my name coming up inside that shit.

As soon as I made that statement, my phone rang. I pulled it from my cup holder, spotting Stanley’s name.

“What’s up, Stan man, what it do?” I answered without hesitation.

“I need to have a word with you, bro, like today!"

“What’s going on, bro, is everything good? I can pull up right now.” I played along, but could hear the tension in his voice.

"Everything is good, but I need you to stop by in like the next hour. I'm having a mandatory meeting."

I wanted to toss the decision out of my head because honestly, it sounded like a setup, but I chose to hold strong until I couldn't anymore. "I'll be there."

Hanging up the line, I tossed it inside my glove box right before I reached M.T.'s street. I was not only in deep with both of these fools, but I was so incognito with hustling that I managed to catch a deal with working off both of their batches of potent dope. I didn't give a fuck about either one of them, and regardless, my plan was to have them eventually clash heads to erase two birds at once. It would leave me snatching the streets of Athens, along with both of these niggas' bank accounts to go with it. The whole mixture of chaos at one time was about to make my rage shatter. It was wild how I had just gotten a call from M.T. and less than ten minutes later, Stan was screaming the same shit through my hook to pull up.

I turned into his driveway, a one story, cream-colored home that he used strictly for moving weight. Jumping out, I knocked on the door, and a quick thought hit me. I was gonna slide up to Thomasville projects to pick me up a set of eyes to watch my back out in Athens. I didn't have another chance to slip with my life or position.

M.T.'s door opened and I locked eyes with his closest guard, Titty Head. His mug was stuck on his face as if it was drawn on with a marker. A large .45 automatic was in his hand as he stepped to the side to let me in.

The vibe inside was calm, and four of his workers and Freaky sat in the living area as he paced around with a large bottle of Patron, sipping it after evert few steps.

"M.T., I got here as soon as I could, big dawg. I don't really know what's going, but just tell me what to do?" I asked with the lie sliding right off my tongue.

I could see he was furious, but I didn't know if it was with me, or if one of his own slipped up and did something that wasn't about to go unanswered.

"I'm glad to see you made it. You know I only call when I really need something important or business handled. I just so happened to slide through Bishop Park today, and my feet ran across ya man Stanley and his crew. Not only did I clash with him, I lost all mercy and respect that I had in my soul to not kill him in public. Now I'm to the point where I want everyone around him dead: workers family, bitches, even parents.

I could tell by the menacing look in his eyes that he wasn't trying to play around, nor was he cutting any emotions on what he wanted done. I knew that my secret was only gonna stay hidden for so long with all the chaos that was surfacing around our hoods.

"So what do you need me to do, big homie?" I asked, wondering what the fuck I was there for.

Pulling a Glock from his hip, he looked around the room, taking a deep swig of the liquor in his hand. His eyes rolled back over to me before he spoke.

"I need you to do the killing. Me and my team are too hot, and the last time I was about to pull a stunt, I nearly had two detectives about to explain exactly how it was about to go down ten minutes after. I'm not trying to lose, but I don't want to win and then lose after if you understand what I'm saying."

"To be honest, I don't," I replied to see if he would cut the sideways talking.

He took a few steps towards me. I stood firmly without blinking. His face was twitching lightly, and I didn't feel any sign of coolness between us at that moment.

"I mean, you're gonna take his team down one by one until they're all dead. I want him ate, and I mean to the fucking bone. You get my drift now?" His voice trailed off like he was more at me than Stanley.

Instead of speaking my true mind on how I felt about the unnecessary aggression, I remained silent and kept all the hostility caged behind my chest. Smiling with a calm posture, I held out my hand.

"Whatever you say, big homie."

M.T. looked down at my hand, walking away smoothly.

"Titty Head, make sure he makes it to his car. We got more business to attend to."

I wanted to pull my gun out and kill everything moving in the crib, and the way Titty Head slid behind me, moving to the door, I knew that the line was behind crossed as an associate for this nigga.

Making it back to my car, I climbed in the driver's seat and backed out of his driveway. Titty Head watched me damn near until I was halfway up the street.

It was more than just two drug kingpins battling for position. They were shooting for death, and M.T. had just put me directly in the center of it.

Chapter 13
Stanley Gerald

Two pistols occupied my hands as I walked around my large backyard in deep conversation with my team, the niggas who I trusted with my life and also the men I fed on a daily basis. It wasn't do doubt in my mind I had loyal men that cherished rising in the game with me, but it was also known now that it was a snake in the grass around my way. I didn't care about the fact of a motherfucking skimming a li'l paper every now and then, but putting my life in jeopardy for the cause of an enemy was were the line had to be crossed.

"Every man standing here, I have given my all, at whatever cost, but today is last stop for someone at this station. I want answers, and I want them now." I gazed around at all my shooters one by one.

My eyes landed on Chip Knock coming out of my home into the backyard. My guard Slim was walking beside him, head hung low as if he knew something that I didn't. He walked directly over to me, and stepped inside the section with the rest of my men.

"Glad you could finally make it, but I can't guarantee that you're here for a good reason. I mean that for everyone standing in this backyard." I alerted him with the truth to see his reaction.

His eyes shifted as if he grew angry immediately, and it still didn't faze me to believe any one just yet. I knew the men that I had around me, but I couldn't tell what was in their heart. It led me to do the only thing I was good at. To go with my first mind like my father taught me when I first stepped foot into this game.

"No disrespect, Stanley. I'm only here on the strength for you. I was asked for my assistance, and I showed up. My day hasn't been so great either, but I still made it my business to get here, so if you don't mind telling me what the fuck going on, we can get on with whatever this is," he replied back to me.

"Today I ran into this fool M.T., and it was crazy because no one knew that we would be chilling at Bishop Park for the Fourth. This nigga pulled up like he was invited by invitation. I know that someone in this yard is the cause of that slip-up, and I know my mind is made up on who that individual is. You see, in this game, you got two types of niggas, ones that have loyalty, and ones that have never known what the fuck loyalty is. It's something that has never been accepted on my side of the field, and it's not about to start now."

All of them were standing still, looking as if they were wondering where my mind was going with the conversation. I wanted to see where the flaw was in my foundation, and I wanted it to disappear like the wind. Raising my pistol to Slim's head, I pulled the trigger before he had a chance to speak or blink.

The sound of my Glock roaring shifted a few of my men's posture, and the blood from Slim splattered recklessly over Chip Knock's clothes and arms. He was standing wide-eyed with a blank face. I knew my action made him nervous because he slowly looked down at Slim's body crumbled up by his feet. I got a tad bit closer to where he was the only one that could hear my words.

"I hope you ain't got no nasty plans in your head, Chip. I'm not getting the same vibes from you, and that ain't like us. I need you to handle this for me, and I mean fast. After that, we can live like kings."

"What the fuck you want me to do, Stanley? This ain't no beef that's got nothing to do with me."

Shrugging my shoulders, I gave him the straight up truth. "Because you're somewhere in the mix, and I can smell it. I trust you, Chip, but that doesn't mean you won't do the quick flip and shade me out. If it's my problem, it's yours too."

He held his hand out, as if my words didn't need to be repeated.

"I got you, big dawg. Just be easy."

I squeezed his hand, burning a hole through his pupils to see if any flaws flew in the midst. Once I felt satisfied, I allowed him to walk out of my yard. Once his car left my home, peeling off into the wind, I made the arrangements to have his life taken immediately after the mission was complete. It was just business, and business always preceded friendship.

* * *

Hallmark Trailer Park
Athens, GA
7:30 p.m.
M.T.

After my dispute with this nigga Stanley Gerald, I made a call to my weed connect, Mark-D. I was picky when it came down to buying anything I put into my lungs. I had replaced my all-white Yukon with a four-door, smoke grey 1990 Jaguar. Once the sun was ducking below the horizon. I was making my way around Classic City for one objective: to build me a team for war.

Sliding inside of Hallmark Trailer Park, I noticed D-Mark's dark tinted Chevy parallel parked as if he owned the entire territory. Freaky and Titty Head accompanied me, just in case I happened to run across my opposition again. I never worried about anyone harming me, but still and all, I never underestimated no motherfucker when it came to surviving in this game.

Pulling in next to Mark-D's car, I watched his window roll down, and his black ass flashed me a huge smile, flexing his gold grill. We weren't too close, but when I needed severe problems taken care of, I knew that I could count on my guy to toss me in the right direction.

"Marlon, wassup, my boy? You don't shop early in the morning, unless you on the lurk for somebody, or you chasing one of them hoes. What the hell you got going on?" he asked me, trying to read my movements.

I looked back at Freaky and Titty Head and wanted to step out of the car to speak more discreetly.

"Do you mind hollering at me alone?" I asked before the conversation could take off any further.

"Come on, M.T. You know I don't move from the comfort of my front seat. I gotta be ready in case the inevitable happens. Piggies don't play around this neck of the woods. I can definitely hear your perfectly from here," he said before tossing me two ounces of the octane through my driver's window.

I flicked him the few bills, wrapped in a rubber band, and sat back in my seat.

"I know you a stand-up man, Mark. That's why I asked you to meet with me. I didn't just pull up for some' to smoke, so I guess I'll cut straight to the chase. You remember that thing you helped me out with a while back, out in Tucker, Georgia?"

"Yeah, what about it?"

"I think I need some more assistance. I need some nigga that's gonna show exactly how mad I am. Do you think that's possible? Because I'll surely make it worth your while." I held up two more grand, flaunting it like a brand new job.

Once he held his hand up in the air, I knew that the ball was about to be rolling. I tossed the extra dough into his lap through the window and watched him spark up a Grand Optimo.

"Tell me who you need, and what you need done?" he replied with a blank expression.

"Stanley, and anybody else that's in a twenty-mile span from that busted-ass nigga. I'm willing to pay double if it's done real special for me. I need a front page news article. If you can't handle it, let me know?" I shot at him to see where his mind was.

At the end of the day, nobody was off limits with the treacherous shit I was about to release on the town, even close ones. I wasn't gonna stop at nothing until I buried every fool that over stepped their welcome within the last month.

"Its gonna cost you fifty G's, M.T. This ain't nothing I allow myself to get involved in because the feelings are mutual with y'all, my guy. I have ties on that side as well, but business is business. I'm not the one pulling the fucking trigger. How fast are you trying to see this happen?"

"Immediately," I replied when he finished his sentence. "Send me a few animals that know how to shake the city up for a few answers of my own. After that, you can send the cleanup crew in to spill everything in their course. Understood?" I questioned to ensure that we were both of one accord.

"Say less. I'll be in touch," he replied while rolling back up his window.

***

Detective Foster
Medical hospital, 2nd Floor

It was around 10:05 when I trailed down the hallway of the medical facility and stopped at the clerk's desk. Wiping the beads of sweat from my forehead, I took a deep breath. The A/C in the waiting area was malfunctioning, and every doctor that I approached about the status of Ms. Williams seemed to brush me off. A white male dressed in black slacks, a white overcoat, and sporting a pair of dark-framed glasses on his face locked in on my badge and stepped to me, hand out.

"Excuse me, sir, are you Detective Foster?"

"Yes, I am. I've been sitting so long that I nearly forgot who I was myself. Is there any good news that you can give me about Ms. Williams?" I asked humbly.

"She has two broken ribs, a fractured skull, her jaw is broken, and forty percent of her body is horribly bruised. She's lucky to be alive, and when I say that, I mean literally. We're gonna have surgery scheduled for her as soon as possible. I can't say that she will recover instantly, but she is awake to the point where she can be coherent to your words if a conversation is necessary. I can only allow you five minutes. State policy."

"That's fine, sir. I'm just glad that she's awake. Any amount of time with her is good as any," I responded with a firm handshake.

I followed behind him as he led me down the hall to room sixteen. "I'll be waiting out here if you need me."

"Thanks, I should be fine."

Heading inside, I paused, witnessing Ms. Williams laying on the stretcher, bandaged and patched as if she was set ablaze. Numerous tubes ran throughout her body, and the beeping sound only made it creepier, as if the devil was sitting in the room with us.

Stepping up to her bed, I looked down and watched her eyes slowly open. She gazed up at me as if she wanted to cry, but I knew that the pain she was experiencing made a lot of her movements impossible.

"Hi, Ms. Williams. My name is Detective Foster with the Athens PD. I'm here regarding what happened to you and your son Jameel. Are you able to hear me?"

It took a good minute, but after standing over her for a certain amount of time, she mustered up her energy to speak. "Please tell me my son is still alive" she asked in a shaky tone."

Her words tore straight through me, and I knew there was no other pain like hearing the seed you birthed was taken and nothing had been presented to tell you whether they were alive or not. A tear fell from her right eye, and I wanted to place every word she spilled under my comfort. It just hurt me even harder that I didn't have the answer at the time.

"I'm not sure, Ms. Williams, but I'm here working night and day to see. I can assure you that I will bring your son home, and I will bring whomever did this to you and Jameel to justice. Is there anyone close to Jameel that would know somewhere he could be during emergencies? Like his hangouts, or secret girlfriends?" I asked, trying to dig for whatever I could.

"Elmadi, he's my son's friend. If anyone knows, he might," she whispered, closing her eyes for a brief second.

I grabbed the phone quickly, alerting the captain of the department for a search warrant. It was clear to pull down on a few shit starters on my list. I was bound to run across more rats and fuckers that placed this shit together.

"Ms. Williams, what school does Jameel attend?"

"Cedar Shoals."

Her response didn't surprise me even though his home was in a totally different area. The crazy part was that I usually spotted him around Clark Central on different occasions. It didn't take me long to realize that I had a high school dropout attending another school where he didn't belong.

Glancing down at my clock, I saw that it was past 10:25, and I wasn't about to waste any more time that was ticking away.

"Ms. Williams, I need you to hang on and hear me clear. I'm gonna put this situation to rest for you and anyone involved is about to fall harder than a stone from Mount Rushmore."

I turned to leave the room and noticed the male doctor still present outside of her room. I wasn't big on trusting, but the man in front of me carried himself with enough good character for the small time that we'd met.

"You make sure no one knows she's here unless it's the authorities. There is no immediate family, so if anyone asks, give them a different name, and contact Athens PD for me," I instructed him before handing over my card.

"Yes sir."

Walking towards the elevator, I prepared myself to hunt down a criminal. For some reason, I knew that the lucky man was gonna be a known killer that I had been waiting patiently to put to rest. My job, my soul, my life, and a teenager depended on it.

Chapter 14
Stanley Gerald

"Damn, Febee," I grunted as she went down on me. For the past twenty minutes I received some of the best head and pampering that any man could ask for, but my mind was still roaming.

Febee bobbled her head slowly, making sure to ease all my tension, and it was more than needed. I massaged her nipples gently through her Gap T-shirt and closed my eyes until she finally made me spill everything I had to offer left in me. I watched her keep it clean and professional, and she raised her head to look at me after it was over.

"Why you act like you not interested tonight? Is it another bitch?" she asked with her breasts dangling freely and hand up to her hip.

I lifted up slowly, trying not to bump the hard-ass cast on my arm against anything. Even after hours of everything blowing over, I could still taste the dried blood that was sticking to my lips.

"Nah, it's not like that, Febee. Work has just been kind of hectic. I'm just trying to line a few things up." I brushed off her question, clearing my throat loudly.

"Boy, that line was faker than a pair of Air Force ones in the flea market. You can't mask that bad-ass attitude for nothing. Is it anything I can help you with?"

Unless she was ready to pull a triple homicide, I knew it wasn't shit else she could assist me with, besides laying against me when I was lonely. "I'm afraid it ain't, li'l mama. This the streets, queen, a dog world, and it ain't no place for you to be jumping in."

Coming to sit beside me, she grabbed my chin, forcing our eyes to lock. "You know the streets aren't something that has to come with you Stanley. You've had scholarships to college, plenty of job offers. The entire Athens loves you, and that's not just because of the packs you drop off on the blocks. It's because you hold family hospitality and loyalty. You can leave when you want and people will still see you the same, Stanley."

"That's bullshit, Febee. Everything that I've ever worked for came out of these streets. I put my all into hustling out there in the hood because I know I'm gonna wake up and nobody gonna give me shit. That's the real part about the block, ma. It never shows love, no matter what you put inside it. You just gotta be prepared to take the losses and snatch your gains as you go. The only thing that's guaranteed is envy!" I yelled, standing to my feet.

Pacing over to my closet, I stepped inside, grabbing my Glock .357, placing it on my hip. "I'm not gonna crash us, Febee, I promise, but I can't just sit back and let a nigga kill us. If it's smoke and I gotta clear the smoke until I calm the animosity, then so be it."

Walking out of my bedroom, I made my way down the flight of stairs until I reached the bottom floor. The beige marble floors sparkled from the gold chandelier dangling from the ceiling, and every inch of furniture and linen was laced with nothing but the best of foreign fabrics. I valued my accomplishments that had been doused on me in the past few years. I was just trying to make sure it lasted. Stepping into my living room, my eyes landed on my three loyal goons, sitting quietly. All attention shot straight to me once I was recognized. Moving over to Pooleg, I embraced him with a handshake.

"You know why I hit you, and I don't wanna keep you boys too long. I hate problems, and we all know problems come in all types of forms and shapes. I'm not the type of man that likes to deal with the differences. I want action -

unmerciful action. Create whatever mess you choose, and bring back the bread in the process. We all split fifty-fifty." I crossed my hand over the hard cast, looking at all of them.

"You really wanna do this with M.T.?" Kevin butted in before Pooleg could speak.

I respected all of them individually, so the question wasn't taken with no disrespect. Fear of a man was the easiest way to catch to blows to the jaw from my pop when I was younger, so being a wimp was scared out of me a long time ago. It was all engraved in my head. I still knew that Marlon wasn't a man to be tested or taken for granted on the turf.

"I'm more than sure, Kevin. I'm positive. We fight fire with fire until the other fire calms. Then we can try to start speaking on coming to peace. Go and check on Rico at the stash spot, get him to ride with y'all if necessary. That understood?" I asked to be sure that I was heard clearly.

"Crystal." Pooleg smiled and headed for the door.

Kevin stood behind him, and my last hitta Butta followed until I was standing in my living room alone.

I couldn't even act as if I wanted to respond about the truth on how I felt about it. All I knew is whatever was behind the weak-ass turmoil I was going through didn't matter anymore. I was just ready for the games to begin.

* * *

Cedar Shoals High School
Elmadi

After listening to the whack-ass social studies teacher give his boring lecture he was dishing out, I nearly blew a head gasket. My schedule was extra tight for today, and it was only the third period of school, around the afternoon time to be more specific. Hearing the bell sound off, I knew that was my time to hightail the fuck out of the class. Not only did Eric and Stacy want to meet up about a new move in progress, but I also had to meet up with my mama to talk first. It was only a few more days before I moved out of the house into my own spot, and I was trying to make sure that she was comfortable by all means necessary. I was earning my way in the world, and I was gonna mandate that my mom was going to be established by any means.

Breezing down the hallway, Stacy caught up to the side of me.

"What it do, ball head? You ready to make this loot next weekend or what?" He grinned from ear to ear. Reaching my locker, he stopped with me as I grabbed a few a few things out.

"Yeah, I am, but I need to do my homework first. I'm not just trying to rush into anything."

Grabbing what I needed, I quickly stuffed it into my Guess jeans. Tossing my bookbag inside, I turned to face him. "I want the money without going to jail, Stacy. Plus patience is a virtue. We could blow it all for trying to be impatient," I added before locking my box.

The sight of a man dressed in a dark black suit caused my flesh to crawl. My eyes shot down to the detective badge on his belt, and before I knew it, I was being thrown back against the locker for a frisk down.

"Mr. Glade, is it? How you doing, young man? Sorry to approach like this, but it seems that you can't even be careful with school kids today." He spoke sternly after shaking my pants leg as if we were on the block.

"Uhh, what the hell is all this about? I'm in a school hallway." I shot him a nasty mug.

Stacy tried his best to pull off, but got stopped in his tracks before he could make two steps.

"Hey blacker than me, hit your ass against the wall before I hit you with a little Georgia power." He pointed at the taser on the other side of his hip.

Following orders as his was told, he grabbed ahold of the wall next to me. It wasn't in my thoughts to be running into the police on the way to lunch break, but sure enough, here I was caught down bad.

"It's funny that I was able to catch you two boys together. I'm actually on the roll with a list of my hard asses, and you two are at the top. Luckily, I only want to ask a few questions, and y'all can be right on about your way."

I exhaled a sigh of relief hearing his statement. I didn't need him digging any further, especially when I had a loaded .38 snub nose inside of my book bag.

"What can we help you with, sir? 'Cause to be honest, I'm lost." I turned to look him in the eyes.

"Your friend Jameel… Did he have any reason for anyone to wanna hurt him or his family? Some bad things took place over the last seventy-two hours, and we want to prevent anyone else from being involved in something much worse."

The questioning of Jameel made my heart slick jump. He still hadn't been found, but I knew the folks was out and about in search of the attackers. I was still lost on exactly what happened. Even though I knew the stunt Jameel pulled, I couldn't say shit. "No sir, none that I'm aware of. Jameel is my friend, but lately he has been distant. He started to hang alone. I felt he needed some space, so I let him be. That's all. Is something wrong?" I asked like I wasn't aware. I was trying to check the radar of this cop's mental, but it was clear that he was already inspection ready. He wasn't searching around for answers. He was searching for a fall guy.

"You wouldn't have any reason to lie to me, would you? This is a critical investigation right now. All form of misinformation can lead to one of you little retards slapped in my cuffs. This doesn't smell like a blank trip to me, so I wanna be accurate when I roll off of this property."

I could see the crookedness in his pupils, and I didn't want anything to do with answering questions for the police.

"Sir, it wouldn't matter if you leave from this property with sixty kids in cuffs. You wouldn't be able to get not one to vouch that I'm involved in whatever mess that has occurred. This is stupidity, I mean even discussing this."

He stared down at me with a vexed expression, one that said I was probably on the shit list with the Athens PD, a situation that I didn't want over my head. He spun the cuffs around his fingers, eyeing us both with spite. The officer could tell that he'd lost the battle for now.

"I want you boys to know that I am the eyes, the ears, the voice, the fucking adjudicator for Athens. This is Classic City for a reason, fellas. So when I take you down, throwing you under the bricks of hell, you'll be remembered just for what you are, son. A fuck up! Now both of y'all yella belly punks steer far from sight, 'cause I'm on your ass like a pair of pockets." He smirked with a pointed finger, walking off.

"What in the fuck was that?" Stacy glanced over to me in confusion.

"I don't know, and I'm damn sure not trying to find out."

I immediately headed to lunch, and by the time I hit the cafeteria, the urge came over me to get the hell out of the school, or I might not make it home by the evening. Heading in the opposite direction, I made my way quickly out of the school's entrance on my own mission.

Chapter 15
Westside of Athens
Li'l Gary

I was never down for snitching on a nigga to see his downfall, but after being shot and kidnapped by M.T., he tossed me out on the expressway at 40 miles an hour. Luckily for me I didn't get hurt too bad, and the police happened to come snatch me up just in time before I bled out. Just as I thought my life couldn't get any worse, I find myself running back into the same detective that I went incognito with a few weeks back. Even after staying days in the hospital, he continued to show until I eventually broke. Now I was left with no choice but to cooperate with the pigs about the murder of Aliyah. True, I hadn't given up a name of a killer, but the thirty years they were offering me for a party to a crime and false information was able to change that quicker than a breath of a newborn.

Posted at the local Waffle House on the west side down the street from my home, I watched Detective's Foster's unmarked Crown Victoria pull smoothly into the parking lot. I hated the fact of dealing with the police to skip out on a bid, but it was me over everything, and taking time for a bunch of niggas I wasn't even sure if I would be around forever had to be crossed out.

"I see you showed up this time. Good. I just wanna let you know that this will look good on you if you decide to go all the way through court for this job with us." He spoke in a moderate tone as he stopped in front of my table.

If my mind was truly on my freedom, then I would've caught the last smart-ass remark that he had made. The shit was just making me hotter than a firecracker, and it was no telling who the hell was laying in the cut, snapping photos of me and this dumb-ass white man trying to oppress me out of info. Instead, everything was slipping right through my ears.

"I don't think it's wise to try and set up a bunch of hooligans in the streets if I'm not playing in them, sir, no disrespect. But you about to get me fucking killed if anybody finds out about this. I mean with two to the back of my head killed. Do you know how that feels?" I stressed, flashing him a serious look for my pain to heard and understood.

This idiot wasn't gonna be able to help me if I was found riddled with bullets on the side of Katherine's Kitchen. It was the trick of all tricks. Allow the cops to catch you slipping, and then they force you to come swap to their side. Now they were the ones pimping.

"I can guarantee you one thing. I might not care who you are, or what you've done to deserve any sympathy for yourself, but I can promise you, I will not let you die. Not on my watch. You'll have twenty-four hour security with you at all times to watch over you. We might not be seen, but we we'll be there. Plus this tracker will always make me aware of where you are in case things get sticky to the point where you can't speak. Understood?" he asked, pushing the 45. shades up on the bridge of his nose.

I wanted to buck like a wild stallion, but I knew that wouldn't have been in my best interests, so I obliged.

"Yeah, that all sounds good and all, but what the hell do you expect me to do? I don't even know M.T., nor do I hang with any of his associates. Where is my whole role for any of this, besides dying?" I shot back

"Because you're gonna make your way from the smallest to the tallest. I need anybody you hang with from Cedar Shoals to speak about what occurred that night of the graduation party to Aliyah. Just follow what I told you, and things will go smooth and perfect.

His speech sounded like a thirsty cop looking for everybody he needed on his new conviction list. I just needed to make it and fake the show until I had a chance to slide out of town. I shook his hand to seal the deal.

* * *

Stanley's Stash spot
Oak Apartment complex
Kevin

It was early when I pulled inside of Stanley's apartments where his spot resided. Instead of me coming through last night, me, Pooleg, and Butta ran into a small problem with one of M.T.'s men and had to trade a few bullets. It wasn't until later on that night I realized I never went and picked up the count up for yesterday like Stanley had asked.

Grabbing the spare key he had left me under the flower pot, I used it and headed inside. Upon walking through the threshold, I heard Rico's voice as if he was speaking to someone on the phone. Instead of me rushing into the living room, I sat back for a second to listen.

"No, that's not what I'm saying, fool. I never wanted to get in the mix of these nigga's business. If you ask me, I'd just rather they kill each other and just get it over with."

Hearing him speak like that, I knew he couldn't have been referring about no one but Stanley and M.T. I made my way closer, still listening closely to him.

"It wouldn't matter who kills who, my nigga. I'm the one with the biggest problem, because I killed Aliyah. That's the only thing M.T. is worried about, and right now all the fingers is pointing at Stanley with the negativity he's adding on. I just think my name is somewhere in the mix and don't wanna take any chances.

Hearing the statement about him being the killer of Aliyah, I made my way around the corner into the living room and locked eyes with him. When he saw my nasty expression, his face changed, and he didn't hesitate to hang up the phone.

"Kevin, goddamn, my nigga, you sneaking up on mu'fuckas now?" He tried to brush me off, standing to his feet. "I got the count for last night. It's upstairs."

My hand grabbed him by the chest, freezing his steps. "So you mean to tell me the entire time we've been wondering where this beef's been coming from, you've been the one masking it this whole time?"

"What the fuck are you talking about, li'l guy? Get the fuck out of my way!" he replied.

"I'm talking about M.T. You killed Aliyah, and this entire line of bullshit is going on right now because of you. Tell me what I heard you just saying on that phone was a lie?"

His face turned into a sinister smile. "Come on, Kevin. We work for Stanley. You mean to tell me that you got some feelings about this little bitch dying too? It was a fucking accident."

"Who the fuck were you talking to on the phone?"

Something told me to push off and let Stanley know exactly what was said instead of alerting this idiot. Right when I didn't expect it, he was rushing towards me, swinging recklessly. One of his fists connected with my right jaw, stumbling me severely. I forced myself to stay on my feet and wrestle with this fucking nigga. He was stronger than he looked, and before I knew it, we were both falling backwards through the glass table, sending shards flying across the room.

We tussled like two pits, and my mind was thinking about the pistol tucked on the side of my hip. As I tried to go for it, both his arms locked around my neck like a Bernese python, stopping all the air in my lungs. My fingers shot to his firm grip, trying to force his ass to let me go, but he was holding on for dear life. I could feel the pressure tighten on my neck and my weak arm tried to reach down once more for my pistol. As I felt my index finger graze against the handle, he landed a hard shot to my temple, knocking me slightly unconscious.

By the time I woke up, Rico Curry had the bag of yesterday's count strapped around his back and my pistol was resting in his hand as he moved around, wiping down certain furniture with a white rag and gloves. I noticed when my vision cleared that I was still laying in the shattered glass, weak as a limp dick. I couldn't even muscle up the energy to lift up.

Rico finished his objective with cleaning his prints and turned back around to face me.

"Damn, Kevin, why you just couldn't keep your damn mouth closed and got you some money? I've always liked you, big dog, but it's just too good to be true with you hearing me speak about what you heard today. Must have just been bad timing on my end. I can't afford for that little secret to get back to anybody. See, I fucks with Stanley, but I also fucks with M.T. In order for me to stay in the clear and let these fools do it to each other, I need all witnesses to remain quiet, if you get my drift," he said to me calmly, checking the barrel of the gun.

I didn't want to panic, but I knew how slim niggas like Rico got down. If I couldn't stress my position of whose side I was on right then, I wasn't about to make it out of the crib alive.

"Rico, I don't give a damn about what you've did. But don't you think it's smart to let the nigga who we working for at least know to kill all fuckery? You're a part of our team, fool. You mean to tell me you're willing to kill me on the strength of some shit with M.T.? Nigga, we could've both went on a mission to kill his ass together. But where's the loyalty in doing this to me or Stanley?" I questioned, trying to get him to change his mental state.

Standing a few feet away from me, he hunched down, laughing hysterically. His eyebrows slanted like the devil himself before he gave me the dirtiest response that I could be given.

"None of you niggas were never meant to last – not Stanley, not even M.T. At first it was just a bad mix up that I placed myself into, but as I started to go on through the days, I seen how this shit could actually benefit me more if I just played these idiots against each other. I could collect all the loot in the end and place the same press these niggas did over these fake-ass dealers that claim to run the block.

"You know it won't be long before somebody kills you, stupid. You think everybody around these boys coming up dead will just go unnoticed?"

I didn't want to tell him that Stanley sent me over to pick up the count because he hadn't really been feeling Rico's vibe for the past few days. It was too late to hide his slime ways, but the info was only ammo.

"It's okay, Kevin. Whoever steps to me, I'll be waiting, and when I say waiting, I mean for anyone that gives me the slightest idea that I'm even being watched too hard. They won't even make it to see Mama's dinner."

"And what about me? You ain't got enough heart to let me be. You don't have to worry about me saying shit. I'm already stuck in trying to clean this up. I should have a little sympathy, my guy. Let me go back to my family."

He stared at me quietly as if he were really weighing the option in his head. Just as I thought he might consider letting me walk, he shook his head and raised the gun up to my head.

"I'm sorry, Kevin. If I let you slide, my man, that means I'll have to let everyone slide. I'm just gonna go ahead and slide around on who I need to until this small problem is no more. You were always a good flunky though, my nigga."

The sight of him wrapping his finger around the trigger forced me to close my eyes before the first shot rang out in my ears.

Chapter 16
Rico Curry

Wiping the last of Kevin's blood from the bottom of my shoes, I grabbed everything worth value along with the money. It wasn't my intended day on flipping the script on the ones that I was just sliding for, but money was sitting thin, and thoughts were starting to turn into conversations. I had to make all my next moves my best one, because I wasn't dying for either side. I was doing it for me.

After leaving the apartment out in the Oak, I climbed inside my black box Chevy, cranking my engine. Swerving out of the apartments, I got half way down the street, and nearly flipped my car from what happened next. An unmarked Crown Victoria blue lighted me. It looked like feds, or maybe ATF. Being sure not to panic and blow myself a trip down to chain gang, I pulled over slowly and stopped my car.

My mind started to rush back on anyone spotting me coming out of the spot, or maybe hearing the gunshots. I watched a white male in a black suit step out. He cuffed the handle of his gun and walked hastily to my driver's window, tapping the glass impatiently.

"Roll it down, right now!"

Huffing all the negative energy out of me, I did as I was told, letting the window sink. I didn't want to look him in the face to get a nasty reaction, so I kept my eyes forward on the road while asking my question. "What seems to be the problem, Officer? I'm just coming from dropping my child off at her mother's place. Is there a problem?" I was sure to keep my hands visible on the steering wheel.

"Mm-hmm. I'm afraid there is, Rico. You have a tag that's expired on your car, not to mention the taillight that's out as well. You mind showing me a copy of your license and registration?"

He was trying to cut straight to the chase, and I could tell out the corners of my eyes that he was watching me like a hawk in the sky. Pulling the papers from my glove compartment, I handed them over, sighing with aggravation. It was my luck to get free picked right after shooting Kevin three times in the head. This wasn't the moment for me to battle it out with an officer because I was gonna make sure I won the war by any means. I had to much on my agenda.

Tossing my wallet and registration card into my lap, he mugged me with a nasty expression. "I hope you know that we see you, Mr. Curry. Your name is hotter than grease with a pot of Chinese chicken. I'm on a hunt for all the scamming lowlifes that have been causing tragedy in my streets, and I'm on it. You might wanna stay cleaner than a douche pouch, punk. I'm at you with every step," he spat, cutting his eyes to the bag on my back seat.

I was hoping he didn't ask anything stupid, because showing him ten thousand in cash was definitely out of the question and would put the radar on a thousand before he let me slide away from the spot I rested.

"What's in the duffle?"

"Workout equipment sir. I was about to head to the gym until you stopped me."

He balled his face up, but stood up straight to shake the light dust from his suit jacket. "You're not gonna know what hit ya until I'm devouring you in the courtroom. You make sure you drive safely now!" he said as I put my car in drive.

Picking up a small bit of speed, my mind eased, and I jumped straight back to the thoughts that were main focus on my agenda. Now that I had erupted the fuckery on both of the kings' table, I was coming to do a little cleaning on both sides. I just wanted to stay invisible while doing it.

* * *

East Point, GA
Two days later
Titty Head

It was around 7:45 a.m. when I pulled up in front of my potna's nice-ass three-bedroom crib, inhaling on a fresh Newport. Lately M.T. wasn't stressing nothing but war, and even though I was known from my hood, I still had niggas that was plotting too and wanted me out of the way for the access of a new and younger crew to slide right on in. That was something I couldn't allow to even take place. When things started to come down to critical moments like this, it was time for me to call on some of my realest associates.

The sun had just started to shine, and I was probably the one and only nigga from Athens GA dressed in all black around the Fulton County area, lurking. My timing was perfect, because just as I was pulling up in his driveway, my main man Dreik was stepping out of his front door with his wife and daughter by his side. His bitch wasted no time mugging me when I hopped out of the car and approached them. The feelings were mutual though. I was only there for one purpose.

"Dreik, wassup, fool? Long time no hear. You already on the move this early?" I gave the friendliest expression that I could so as not to startle his bougie-ass wife.

"Damn, dog, long time no see. I was just about to drop the li'l one off at the school house down the street." He embraced me with a brotherly handshake.

Just from the way his wife Cassandra was tooting up her nose, I knew it she was about to throw a fit. “Dreik, we don’t need to be late dropping her off. Is everything okay?" she asked him as if I was just coming to start some trouble.

“Look, baby, go ahead and take her on down to the school. I’ma sit back and catch up with Titty Head for a second and call you when I’m done.”

Her expression said that she wanted to buck, but to my surprise, she grabbed the baby’s hand, leading her to the car. After all, Dreik was more than a friend. He was a brother, and nothing would ever be able to come in between us, not even a nagging-ass baby mama.

Just as she got in the car and drove off, he smiled, gesturing for me to follow him in the crib.

“Titty Head, what the hell I told you about just popping up man. You know Cassandra still hot at you about killing that nigga in front of our home last year. I had to move because of yo’ crazy ass.” He rested down into one of the sofa chairs.

I couldn’t help but to laugh when this nigga spoke because even though he was always willing to go to the extra mile for me, he was uncut when it came down to keeping shit real. No matter what problems a person could think I may cause, Dreik always welcomed me back with open arms.

“I didn’t come to cause trouble, Dreik. Besides, the young nigga shot at you first, remember?”

He nodded in silence, but knew for a fact that my words were sincere and one hundred percent true.

“I need your help, Dreik, and I’m willing to pay you for it." I cut straight to the chase.

Dreik walked over slowly to his mini bar. He poured himself up a drink of Patron. Sometimes it was like he couldn’t think unless he was drinking, like his mind couldn’t process a serious situation unless he drank and pondered on it, especially when dealing with me.

"Li'l bro, I got plenty - let me rephrase that - I got mad love for you. But ya just be a li'l too turned up for me. When we were younger, it was damn near possible to get away with anything, Titty Head. That shit ain't the same no more, plus I got a wife and two kids now that stress me every chance they get."

"Just hear me out first. I'm only here because I know that no one can even think about laying the pistol game down with me like you do. It's damn sho' for a reason."

Reaching down into the tote bag I came with, I pulled out a large portion of cash, setting it on the glass table. I watched Dreik rub his chin before leaning forward.

"How much is it, and where did you get it, Titty Head?"

"It's sixty-three thousand dollars, and the bank just approved me yesterday to open up an animal hospital." I threw out some humor to lighten his ass up.

He chuckled before tossing back the rest of his drink like an elder. He knew that I hated to also be questioned, so I tossed giving an answer right out of the window.

"Like I said, it's three bands. I don't trust a motherfucker to hold three pennies and a dime sack of weed, so I couldn't just pull up on anybody for help. I need you to help me handle a few things out in Athens with me, and I can guarantee you on my end that no drama will come back to you and Cassandra. Plus you'll always eat as long as I'm running around in these streets.

He was evaluating my proposition like bucking was in his vocabulary, but we were the same breed, so denying to step with me was like a best friend leaving his day one for the slaughter. That was a trait that I knew for a fact did not coincide with Dreik not one bit.

"Done," he agreed, holding out his hand to shake mines.

That was one reason I never cut ties with the nigga. He never let me down for nothing. Even though he wasn't too tough on the street shit anymore like he was back then, he would still keep it solid whenever needed. After kicking flava with my nigga for the next twenty minutes and giving him the details of what was ahead, I prepared to leave.

Hopping in my whip, I decided to make my way back to Athens to my little freak's house to pick up my other car. Just thinking about li'l mama made me amp up. That ass was dumb fat, and it had been a minute since I slid up in some tight pussy. Even though she wasn't my main, she respected that a nigga had to pave a way to eat. I considered myself more of a businessman than anything. Getting a job was easy for me. Since the age of fourteen, I was picking up that smoke pole to gain the shit that I needed for school. Eventually I said fuck that and started picking up the heat to take away a dopeboy's bankroll or safe.

I turned the hood of Athens upside down with my press game, and now I was about to show everyone else how the game was laid when a person crossed the wrong boundaries.

Chapter 17
Ben's Sports Complex
Vincent Drive
M.T.

Brushing the blunt ashes from my Louis Vuitton button down, I waited patiently inside of the sports complex, where I usually picked up my loads of white girl. It was a popular spot to make business pop, and anybody who had a name in Athens had their share of pulling up just to make themselves present every now and then. It was just like the wind. If you stay gone a little too long, nobody felt your breeze anymore and you eventually became nothing. I was being sure that muthafuckas still stressed name.

The sky was looking pure and clear, but a few of my emotions was off balance. The mood in the air was funny, and I didn't usually feel like that when I showed up to a place like the sports complex. It was days that would always make me uncomfortable, but I didn't never expect what happened next to ever occur.

"I'm saying Marlon, why it ain't jam-packed around this bitch like any other day? It look thin as hell out here in the parking lot. Like the feds got an eye on this motherfucker!" Pooleg laughed, trying to lighten the tension.

I had been waiting for my plug to pull up for the past ten minutes, and it was never like him to be running behind time.

"Have one of y'all heard from that nigga Kevin or Rico yet? I haven't got a reply since night before last from neither one of them. Y'all said that these were the best niggas to get close to this dude. Now it seem like they catching cold feet. They know how bad I want this nigga Stanley's head, and now nobody picking up a phone? And now that you mention it, yeah, it do seem funny, but you can't expect fools to keep they word when it comes down to linking up with us. Some niggas ain't even meant to be in our presence. It's the cause of all causes, Pooleg. We move how we move for positions and power. That's the reason were still at the top of the food chain, baby boy. I'm not trying to pass that up no time soon."

"True," Butta added in. "Not trying to cut the convo, boss man, but I think this ya guy right here about to pull in now." He nodded towards the two dark blue Impalas pulling inside the sports complex.

I had never witnessed those specific cars upon us meeting in the past, so I truly thought nothing of it. The moment the first window rolled down, I spotted an AK-47 barrel protruding from inside. Things seemed as if they were moving in slow motion as I reached for the pistol on my hip. Before I could even aim, a bundle of shots to let loose violently.

Bloc! Bloc! Bloc! Bloc! Bloc! Bloc! Bloc!

I hit the ground rolling over to my side, letting three shots burst from my chamber.

Poc! Poc! Poc!

Butta was shooting recklessly, clapping back at the two cars of nigga however he could. I couldn't make out any face, but bullets were dancing out the side of my truck, shattering the establishment windows sitting behind me. I let off a few more shots, stumbling back to my feet. Once I started to let the clip ride, the two tinted Impalas were smashing out into traffic, speeding back the opposite way down Vincent Drive.

"M.T., you alright my nigga." Pooleg rushed to my aid, checking for any wounds, as I leaned against the trunk of my truck.

I was still breathing heavily, and the only thing running through my mental was who the fuck were the individuals that just nearly shot me, and how I was gonna deliver a horrible and catastrophic fate for the sloppy attempt on my life?

"Yeah, I am, but I can't say the same for whoever the fuck just pulled up on me!"

Pulling out my phone, I dialed my plug's number, waiting for an answer. The line rang three times before it was picked up.

"Speak."

"I know that I'm not at odds with you, so I'm guessing you don't know about the shooters that just gunned at me in the mix of meeting up with your runner." I spoke closely into the receiver so he could hear every word I said.

"I don't think you would be talking to me if that was a part of my doing, M.T. We are big boys now. I approach beef personally, and never have been fond of sending messages. I leave them. Are you having problems in your own space now?" he asked with a hint of sarcasm leaking from his tone.

I didn't want to crash every avenue in the middle of me being furious, so I decided to ease down a bit until all doors opened to reveal the answers I needed.

"I need to set up a meeting, ASAP!"

"Well, I guess I'll be seeing you soon," he responded, ending our call in one note.

I quickly jumped behind the wheel of my truck. Butta took the passenger side and Pooleg jumped in the back as I cranked the engine to leave.

"Who the fuck do you think is behind this, M.T.? Stanley?" Butta raged.

I never replied or made a negative gesture from hearing dude's name, but in the back of my mind, I wasn't seeing anything but murder. I didn't know exactly what move I wanted to make, but I was for sure about one thing. All mercy was out of my system. Asking questions was officially off my agenda. Bodies were about to fall plentifully on the grounds of Athens.

I wanted all the blood, and I was gonna make sure to shed it out of every bitch that stood against me.

* * *

Chelsey's Strip Club
Elmadi

It had a been a few days. I moved out of my mama's crib into my own spot. I ended up purchasing a two-bedroom home down the street from Rolling Ridge. I didn't want to just up and leave my mama, but I couldn't sit around waiting for some drama to come flying into our crib before I took the advice on trying to duck off and out of my mama's home.

It was already a late Thursday and I was out and about, placing my own set of plans in effect. I had gotten word about a few people that were so-called involved in Andre's murder, and I immediately jumped back into my own investigation. I didn't want to fall victim in the streets from my own curiosity and anger, so I was being sure to line up my choices correctly when it came down to how I was moving.

As I walked inside of Chelsey's strip joint, the music was bumping smoothly through the speakers. A couple of low budget niggas sat around the stage as the voluptuous, gorgeous women moved about, dancing and grinding to the beat. Kilo Ali's single "Baby, Baby" was blasting, and the different exotic girls enticed every big pocket. It didn't take long for me to find who I was looking for. I spotted her bright red olive skin glowing off the hue of the spotlights flashing from the ceiling. I moved coolly through the floor until I reached the other side of the club. Her hair was curled to the middle of her back. Her body was beyond magnificent, and the warm smile she wore let me know that she was definitely related to Diego and Black Caesar.

"Hi Rere," I spoke politely, trying to grab her attention.

As she turned around, her beauty shined harder than a diamond. I was actually starstruck, but remembered that I was there on business.

"Hey there, handsome. You must be E? My cousin Diego told me all about you," she spoke, her hips still moving in rhythm.

"Yeah, he told me to show up to Chelsey's and I would know exactly who you were when my eyes landed on you. I can definitely see that you're related to them." I smirked, gazing up and down at the stallion in front of me

"Come on. Let's go somewhere a little quieter." She grabbed my hand, leading me towards the back where the locker rooms rested.

A few other strippers watched as I maneuvered through the building, but I could sense that I was more than good, being that I was by Rere's side. She led me towards an office in the back of the women's dressing room. I stepped inside behind her and took a seat in a black leather chair.

"You have to excuse my attire. It's kinda like my uniform on a daily." She giggled speaking about the two-piece bikini that was glued to her body.

"Trust me, Rere, it's no problem. To be honest, I'm glad that you agreed to meet with me. I told Diego that I was willing to pay you for your help if necessary."

Taking a seat across from me, she crossed her legs. "That depends on exactly what you need assistance with. I'm able to do a lot of things, depending on the circumstances."

"I need your help finding out who killed my friend, something I'm willing to pay whatever necessary for. The only reason I want to work with you is because the idiot that I got my eye on, his thugs happens to come to Chelsey's often, and just so happens they're always requesting you."

She sat straight up in her seat after I made the remark and I could tell that I hit the hammer on the nail with the info Diego, and Black Caesar were feeding me.

"I guess you're speaking about M.T., Butta, and Pooleg. That crew, huh?"

"What makes you figure?"

"Because usually M.T. and Pooleg are the ones asking for the opposite of what you need. They're usually the ones doing the looking, and I haven't met too many individuals coming inside of Chelsey's looking for anyone that hangs with that circle."

I flashed her a look that said shit could easily change, but I still had to choose my words carefully to know if she could be trusted without pulling any crooked shit that could set me off balance on my plan.

"That could always change, sweetheart. Unfortunately, they're not the only people having money to do what they want, so the dollar speaks volumes over a voice. My main concern is to make sure that I can trust you and that you're safe in the process."

Crossing her arms over her breasts, a scandalous grin formed across her face. "This game is business. You pay for your way. I'm just the chica that wants her coins before I decide to join. What exactly do you need me to do, and how much you talking?" She crossed her legs, tilting her head with emphasis.

I pulled out the couple of grand that filled my pockets. She flashed an inquisitive gaze. That alone let me know that I was finally in effect.

Chapter 18
Jameel

Smelling the alcohol burning through my nostrils, I shook my head, and a large headache immediately erupted around my brain. My eyes gazed around the dark basement that I was sitting in. I noticed that both my hands and feet were chained down to a love seat like I was some type of test project.

M.T.'s shooter Freaky moved around me quietly, grabbing items out of a nearby deep freezer, and a menthol Kool cigarette burned between his lips slowly, as if he was savoring the taste of the cancer. Roaming my eyes down my bloody clothes, I noticed a sewn-up gunshot wound in my shoulder. It looked like a nigga had played doctor on my shit to stop the bleeding, but I was quite confused on everything that transpired. All I could remember was Sky Dog telling me I was dumb for ever taking the chances on playing with M.T.'s rims, and now I was truly regretting it.

I tried to lick my lips from the dryness and speak clear enough for Freaky to hear me.

"Is my mama still alive? Please tell me she isn't dead, man?" I forced my eyes to look at him.

"Holy shit. You're woke. Bitch, you've been passed out for the last four days, and I tried my best to patch you up, as you can see. As far as your mom goes…"

He cracked his neck with a disturbing whistle. It sent chills through my fucking bones.

"That's something you gotta ask the big man." He continued with doing his task.

The statement alone had me ready to cry about my old lady. I hadn't laid eyes on her since that day, and instantly the regret started to flow. I didn't know where I was, and I wasn't sure if I would make it out alive. All I knew is that I would try to do whatever it took to rewrite my days and take Sky Dog's words to heart.

Just when I felt like the day was going to be unquestionably hard, I saw the door to the basement open, and down came M.T. and his killer, Titty Head. He trailed right behind the demon, and all I could do was stare him down until he came directly in front of me and stopped.

"It's about time you got some juice in you, my nigga. I been riding around the city laying the smack down and making back all the hard-earned money that I've lost because of you. It's crazy because I was just shot at today, and still have no valid reason why. But the only thing that can pop up in the back of my head is maybe somebody out here doing it for you. You got some super helpers out there that I need to know about?" he asked, dragging on the rolled blunt that was lit between his fingers.

"I don't know what you want from me, man! Is it the rims? 'Cause I can't get them back ,M.T. I sold 'em. I can tell you who I gave them to. Can you at least tell me if my mother still alive? I accept whatever you gonna do to me man. Just tell me?" I looked him square in the eyes to see if I could read him.

His soul was so demonic and uneasy he actually had the nerve to crack a smile at me. I didn't know if that was my confirmation, but I promised myself one thing. If I was to ever get the cuffs around my wrist to come off, I was gonna try my best to kill him myself. My chances were slim to none, but I made sure to keep it sitting on the back of my conscious.

"I'm sorry, li'l man, you should have thought about the reaction of what could happen to Mama before you stole my shit. See, I believe in being fair. I been that way my whole life, Jameel. I gave you a chance to be fair when I came up to the school, even when I came to the crib, giving you a chance to be truthful, and what did you do? You played the game hurtful. All for a pair of rims. Not to mention all the bullshit I had crawling up my back with my little cousin Aliyah."

My head raised when he mentioned Aliyah. The thought of her being murdered still was a shock to me, but the crazy thing about it was, I knew the guilty man was still moving about freely with no repercussions set against him. That was because the stupid-ass nigga M.T. still had no clue on who pulled the hideous act. That was my chance to take advantage, and throw any nigga under the bus that I felt led this monster to the home where my mother rested her head. That first idiot was Sky Dog, and right behind him was gonna be the dirty nigga he ran his fucking mouth to.

"You worried about a pair of rims, and I've known the entire time who was involved with killing Aliyah. You think the prettiest girl in Cedar Shoals gets murdered and nobody hears or see anything?" I shot the statement in the air with nothing else to lose

I can tell I struck a new line of anger from how his face frowned up. Walking over towards me, he snatched the gun from his hip, dangling it by his side. That alone let me know that I had a new chance to play the ball in whatever field I needed. I was going to do whatever necessary to face the same nigga that threw me under the bus.

"Say what, nigga? If you know anybody that had anything to do with killing my sister's daughter, I think you need to spill every soul possible before I push yo'; shit back into that old chair your head resting against. I hope this not a game?" He slowly raised the gun, placing it against my chin.

My heart was flushing harder than my bowels down a prison toilet, but I had to remain firm if I wanted to get out of that room alive, so I said the first thing that came to my mind. A lie.

"It's obvious, my nigga. I got turned on to your Cadillac by a young one that hangs around the same complex you sneak through. I know Sky Dog sounds familiar. He's just a pigeon in a dog cage because the master mind is the same nigga that was smashing your girl Wanda," I said to see how his face would turn.

He pondered on what I was saying for a slight second before tapping the barrel of his gun across his own temple.

"Tell me you're not talking about Elmadi? The little nigga that's boosting all the hot shit around the city. He's the one that murdered my cousin?" he asked, squinting his eyes.

I forced my head to nod, praying that he just didn't take the anger out on me and blow my brains out.

"What about me and my mother, M.T.? I don't think nobody would've ever gave you a solid confirmation on this since you been on the hunt about it, big bro. Spare me," I requested.

A house phone sitting in the far corner started to ring just as he was about to answer me. I watched him nod to Freaky, and he quickly ran to answer it. Once he picked up, there was a short conversation held with whomever was on the other side of the line. He never replied after speaking the first time, and the way his face balled up, I could sense something else just landed home on M.T.'s table. I just prayed that it didn't slim my chances.

Watching Freaky hang up, he made his way back to his boss side. "M.T., that was Chip. He said they just found Kevin's body out in Oak Apartments. He was killed. I'm guessing everything that was in there with him is gone also."

Rubbing a hand across his mouth, M.T. slowly began to rock with anger and released a nasty yell like he was Tarzan. Veins were protruding from his face and his chest was heaving like an ape. Freaky even had to step back. "Find out who the fuck did it. Locate wherever the fuck Rico is and see what happened. If he can't tell you nothing, shoot his ass in the back of the head," he ordered.

"Understood." Pooleg turned to leave us alone.

M.T. paced in a circle a few times before moving back over to me. "I hope that what you're telling me is solid, because if it's not, after you wake up this time, it'll be receiving two bullets to the center of your head and exiting earth," he said before colliding his gun across my face, forcing me to go unconscious.

Chapter 19
Garnett Ridge Apartments
Stanley Gerald

I used one hand to grip on Keisha's backside as she rode me into satisfaction. Her melon-shaped breasts bounced freely, allowing my lips to gaze her nipples every time she came down on me.

"Damn, li'l mama, keep going," I grunted as she handled the business.

Her luscious lips were cooler than an A/C against my skin, and she was squeezing her muscles, trying to make me release all the pent-up energy.

Flipping her over on all fours, I climbed behind her, slowly entering that sweet spot.

"Ssss! Stanley, slow down a bit." She winced as I sped up a bit.

Her body was so hypnotizing, sweating, and grinding to a rhythm with mines. It was never impure with her whenever we was together. The intense passion we shared allowed my pleasure to rise for her with every second we intertwined. Feeding Keisha a few more long, hard, thick strokes, I ended my session with a mean nut and some light pecks to the back of li'l mama's neck.

We didn't speak after we were done. It was silence, happy silence of my success with the game, and also the new connect that just happened to fall in my arms. It was my world, but I was starting to get uncomfortable, and M.T. was now ninety-nine percent of that dissatisfaction.

"What's bothering you, Stan? You haven't said anything all night. It seems like the only thing I can get out of you is a damn grunt." Keisha faced me, expressing her anger.

I didn't want to be the buzzkill of the night, nor did I want to act like a lame around a piece of pussy. My name was built of the foundation I laid in Classic City, and now it was being tarnished. I was never the type of breed to shed blood with the same nigga we came up around, but the principles and morals that the old heads truly went by just didn't apply anymore to the generation I was coming up in.

"Too much bullshit that's just slowing down my bread. I don't wanna make more of a mess moving off of ignorance, but I can't keep taking to much more of this cutback."

Judging from the way she turned back the opposite way, she wasn't too interested, or just flat out didn't give a damn about what field I was in. I didn't expect her to.

Hearing my cell buzz, I grabbed it from the nightstand and noticed that it was my mother. Tossing my legs over the side of the bed, I slid on my basketball shorts and house shoes to head downstairs.

Breezing down the hallway, I thought about all the wild shit I had transpiring. I was involved with two women that I couldn't break loose from. A full war was in progress, and I was about to be part of one of the biggest federal investigations out of Athens, GA.

Reaching the bottom floor, I used the house phone inside of the kitchen to place my call. I waited patiently, and once I heard her beautiful voice croon through the line, I smiled to myself

"Wassup, Mama? How's ya day going, boss lady?"

"Oh, baby, it's always joyous when I know that you're just a dial away. You know I gotta do my double checkup. You're staying out of trouble ,I hope?"

"You know how that goes, Ma. I gotta make a dollar the best way I can. Yo' bills ain't about to pay they self. That's what Dad used to say, right?"

"Boy, your father took care of us and spoiled you and your brother with certain things just so he could cover up his mistakes. Money never stopped him from putting his hands on me behind closed doors, and it didn't stop him from going up inside other women. When I first met your father, I just knew that I would be with him forever. I was never worried about what was in his pockets, Stan. I just wanted him to stay loyal and treat me like I was the only special queen that actually mattered. Instead, he slept with every tramp he ran across. I sat back and kept my mouth closed for a long time because I didn't want to bring the extra drama around you and your brother. There wasn't a limit when it came down to taking care of y'all, but I suffered through hell to cover up all the falls within our personal life whenever things got out of hand. Now money doesn't mean anything, son. Now if that's the meaning of taking care of your family, you might wanna switch it up real quick."

I took everything my mother said to heart, and I couldn't deny the real. She was absolutely right. Money was the biggest competition when it came down to keeping structure together. It was one of the main things I feared: betrayal from the ones closest to me.

"Why haven't you've ever told me this before?" I asked, leaning back against the kitchen counter.

"Stanley, some things are just left better unspoken, because in this cold world we live in, I learned that one thing is guaranteed, and that's me returning back to my God. Anything other than that is artificial."

"That's right, old lady. I don't know where you getting all this juice from, but you've always had a way of dishing it out to me. I'm more than grateful. Thank you, Queen." I smiled from her warm love.

“Anytime, pumpkin. Just make sure Mama don’t catch no heart attack from any bad news. You all I got left now.” She giggled, warming up my spirit.

“Sure thing, Mama," I added before ending our call.

The inspiration from my mother’s speech not only calmed me, but it prepared me for what was ahead. I had been the head honcho in Athens for a while since I was eighteen, but there was also M.T. adding up his growth right beside me on the other side of town. I didn’t need any unwanted beef, so I had one more choice to offer him. Worrying the woman that birthed me was definitely not a part of my history. But in the end, I was a businessman. In order for business to go all the way accordingly, certain buttons were gonna have to be pushed, and I was about to finally put the buttons in effect.

* * *

Rolling Ridge Slums
One day later
Li’l Gary

After sitting in custody for the past week, Detective Foster was making sure to show me that he was far from playing about throwing me behind the big house if I refused to work as an informant. The long seven days gave me enough time for my wounds from M.T. to heal a li’l better and for me to go ahead and book as many niggas as I could to get this crooked ass cop off my bumper.

So much damage had been caused around Athens since I had got pressed into what I was about to do. The police were a problem, but I was worried more about one of the kingpins finding out about me giving a statement on them both. Using my brain, I decided to start with the foundation and watch the heads fall behind. After I found out that Fredreshia, Crystal, and Joy was throwing a house party for the block, I knew that it was the perfect time for me to pull up and see if I could get the number one grinder under my belt: Elmadi.

"What's good, Li'l Gary? Boy, you been missing in action lately, ain't you?" He looked me up and down.

He was dressed in a black Calvin Klein suit and a pair of white Bally kicks. I could tell that he was doing a little more than the average twelfth grader that was months away from heading to college.

I turned around to see Danny Boy smoking on an Optimo. Joy and Stacy were on the other side of them, engaged in their own conversation.

"Naw, Danny, just a li'l vacation from all this bullshit to see my grams, man. She sick as a dog, so you know how that go. Aye, have you seen Elmadi?" I asked so I could spin his ass out of my face.

"I just saw E about ten minutes ago. More than likely he's inside of Fredreshia's spot where the party is going. You know that fool can't be still."

Turning on my heels, I took his response as the avenue to get the hell out of Dodge. The wire that was taped to my chest was starting to irritate my fucking skin, but I wasn't leaving Rolling Ridge until I knew that someone was about to take this indictment off my plate.

Walking towards Fredreshia's building, I walked inside and noticed that everybody was partying like this is how we do it on Friday night. The young hoes around the room was dancing like it was the last night of fun. You couldn't see the middle of the floor, so I knew that everyone attending had to be somebody important. It didn't take long for me to get into the groove with a few friends. Truly, I was on eggshells, wondering if anybody knew about my affiliations with the police.

Just as the thought was leaving my mental, I took a west back and nearly tripped over someone behind me.

"Goddamn, idiot, watch ya step." I turned to see Elmadi looking at me with a gaze of hatred.

"Naw, fool, I think you need to watch yo' step. You bumped into me, and you scuffed my shoe, Li'l Gary," he said with a nasty tone.

My heart pace slowly sped up during our encounter, and I prayed like hell that the wire on my chest didn't sweat out before I could get him to talk about the fuckery that had taken place at the graduation party.

"My bad, E. You know I don't mean no damn harm, man. It's crazy that I run Into you, because you're just that guy that I needed to see. You mind if I get a moment of your time?"

"Sure, talk," he spat out nonchalantly.

"Come on, E, we better than that. You know how we talk about business. How about we catch the front porch or some'?"

I thought that he was going to reject my request, but he ended up obliging. After we made it to the front of Fredreshia's spot, I pulled a cigarette out my front pocket, offering one to E.

"No thanks. I don't do the cancer thing. So what is it that you were trying to talk about?"

I gathered my thoughts of everything that I had to say before speaking because I didn't want to offset the mood, making myself suspicious. "You're the only nigga I know young and still doing the things that you can do. Of course I've been in the streets too, but never have I had the ambition as you do to get that dough. I wanna be a part of the team. Word is that you got the best crew around Athens boosting whatever they can put their hands on .We all know it ain't too many people around our way doing too much to get that stunt on like Evil

Knievel, but the Rolling Ridge crew has been more self-sufficient, if I do say so."

"Listen, Gary, I don't know what the fuck you talking about. You ask to speak about business, but it seems like you're trying to write an article on someone's life story. Maybe you should just say what's on your mind so we can see where this conversation is going. 'Cause I'm lost," E responded.

He was staring at me curiously, and my palms felt as if they were starting to sweat.

"All I'm trying to do is get with the program, Elmadi. I know you don't trust a lot of niggas. Cool. But you don't trust anybody. So at least just hear my piece, and then I'm out. My folks out here down bad, man. Rent due, and I can barely help my mama feed my little sister, man. All I'm asking for is one chance to straighten my bank account, E. Ever since Aliyah got killed at that house party, it's like my shit has been going down."

I didn't know whether I hit him with too much or just enough, because he grew quiet, staring at me with an unreadable face.

"Maybe you need to try and put in some job applications, Li'l Gary. Athens is dry right now, but if I can run across anything that can assist you in these next few days, I'll let you know," he replied, sliding straight back into the house party, out of sight

The new vibe I was starting to get forced me to push on about my business. It was gonna take more than a day to lay down the plan Detective Foster was trying to enforce. I just didn't know that I would never make it for the story to be told.

Chapter 20
Club Gresham
Toot

The atmosphere in the club was past exquisite tonight. Girls frolicked around the room, and street hustlers and thugs poured up until people started to fall face first on the floor. I was on my fourth blunt and the cocaine that I had just snorted numbed my headache from where Stanley's men tried to blow my head off a few days back. I felt like I was in the fucking Twilight Zone.

Spotting my baby mama sitting at the mini bar, I paced over to her, leaning against the counter.

"Baby mama, where the hell the rest of my powder? And I need you to order me another Patron with ice."

"Toot, your breath smells like shit, and you should've asked that bitch you was just dancing across the floor with. I left that trash-ass cocaine in the side panel of your car seat." She turned with anger, facing the woman on the opposite side of the bar.

Mushing her head with my index finger, I made off to the front entrance and walked past the bouncers guarding the door. It took me a minute to get to my car, but once I reached it, I opened the door, flopping inside in search of the nose candy. As I dug through every part of my whip that I could search, a loud tapping on my hood forced me to raise my head.

Spotting Stanley, Butta, and Pooleg, I nearly shitted myself. There was a slight moment of silence lingering before Stanley walked around to the window on my side of the car. He tapped the glass and I played it smooth rolling it down coolly. The only thing throwing me for a loop was the guns Pooleg and Butta held in their hands. I hadn't seen them since our last encounter, but I could sense they were mad I escaped the bullet that was supposed to take my life.

"If it ain't my loyal man Toot. I never thought that I would run into you again. Can you give me any reason why our last conversation never added up? I been hearing you've been sliding your nose into business that you have nothing to do with. Or maybe I'm just hearing the most?" He shot me a grin that told me he heard the right shit.

"Stanley, I'm not sure what you talking about, but I know nothing but loyalty - the same shit I was stressing the first time yo' men nearly shot my face off. I've never been good with riddles, and your shooters standing in front of my whip holding guns. It don't look like it's just for fun. What's supposed to be up now? Keep it gutta with me." I slowly reached for the .38 in between my seats. I didn't want to go out bad this time, but getting shot was not another mission I wanted over my head.

"It's life, Toot. We can just put it that way, li'l homie. When I first met you, I was excited about letting you be a part of this team for your brand hustle. But word is that you been playing two sides, and I'm not the man for that type of disloyalty. So yes, today is the correct time for you to see just how much of a mistake you've made."

"So you've come to kill me?" My mind was racing like a greyhound around the track for a winning ticket.

"No, I didn't come to kill you, Toot." He laughed as if I was tripping.

I took a deep breath upon hearing his words.

"They came to kill you." He gazed back over to his hounds walking off.

Before I could even speak a word, a gang of gunshots started to rain from their guns into my car.

Chapter 21
Rico Curry

I was sitting in the hotel room, thumbing through the paper I had been collecting over the past few days. Kevin's phone that I confiscated from his body the other day started to ring again. Getting tired of hearing the annoying sound, I finally picked up.

"Yo, who the fuck is this?"

"Well, I can tell by your aggressive attitude that this has to be M.T.! I've been blowing the line loose. I started to think you didn't like bitches anymore."

A woman's voice was booming through the line, throwing me clean off guard. She sounded bad as hell, but the crazy part was her calling me M.T. I already knew by the contacts saved inside Kevin's phone that he was no straighter than me with how he was playing the filthy role. I just happened to beat him to the punch, getting him before he got me. Instead of denying the caller, I decided to play the game how it was dealt.

"Yeah, this M.T. And who might this be?"

"Its Rere from Chelsey's, the same one who you're always requesting whenever you're present. I haven't seen you in a while and decided to do a check-in on the number you gave me a while back. Does that refresh your memory?" she asked through the receiver in a seductive voice.

I almost wanted to laugh, but held my composure. "Of course I do. But what can I do for you on this fine evening, li'l mama? I'm currently wrapped up in some business and wasn't expecting any surprise calls."

"Oh, this isn't a surprise. I'm calling you to put you on game for the plans on your schedule."

"Oh yeah?" I replied, fumbling with a stack of money. "What might that be?"

"Well, I was thinking you could relax and get some great pussy from a true queen after you handle your beef with the man that came to this club paying to find you. Luckily, I had this thing saved with your number in it to give you a friendly warning. If I didn't have your name sitting by it, I would have by passed this entire ordeal. Lucky for you, huh?" she said.

"Oh yeah, that's more than lucky for me. You're an angel, and I might have to definitely take you up on that offer after my business is handled. I'm a man that's not used to being looked for. If you don't mind me asking, did you get a description or a name on how this guy looked?" I questioned, trying to dig further.

I knew for a fact that it was only a few niggas literally bold enough to come in an establishment asking for a nigga like M.T. He wasn't nothing to be fucked with, so if that was occurring, obviously some fuels in the street were being doused with fire through the grapevine. This was my opportunity to do more than gain a check. It was my time to capitalize, to kill two birds with one stone.

"Well, he was average height. maybe six foot. Wavy hair, and looked like he had a bundle of cash to throw. Instead of him giving it to me to shake my ass, he gave it to me for information. Information that involved me setting you up. I think his name was Stanley. Does that ring any bells?"

Hearing Stanley's name was like bells to little children's ears on Christmas Eve. It was literally a blessing in disguise for me to grab this idiot's phone from his body. He was giving me the ultimate play, and I was about to push start on that bitch with no hesitation.

"In fact, I do know that name. I know that name more than well. How about you do me a favor. I'm going to give you a place where you can tell this Stanley guy to find me, and I can handle the rest from there. Once you've done that, it's an easy four grand for you, just for your hot tips that saved a bad man's life. Maybe after that, me and you could link up?" I shot out there just to make it sound better than good.

"Just tell me when and where, and watch me work my magic, daddy."

"Perfect. Look out for the address in a ten-minute span. After that, I would advise you to stay in contact until everything is all over," I lied.

"Your world, your rules, sweetie. You know where to find me," she agreed before ending our call.

I was smiling from ear to ear. My head ran a full mile dash on exactly what I needed to do. Stanley was definitely about to run into exactly what he wanted, and he was probably waiting on M.T's tricks to fail so he could accomplish the same thing: murder. With both of the top gunners in Athens out of my way, it left a clear path for the taking of Classic City, and I wanted a shot at the throne.

Using the phone, I quickly dialed M.T.'s pager number. By the time he made the call to see who was trying to contact him, I was gonna deliver the message and watch the rest unfold before my eyes. I wanted popcorn and front row seats, because whoever thought they were gonna walk away would meet true devil in person right after. Me.

* * *

Elmadi

I was sitting at my kitchen table with Sky Dog, Stacy, and BoRat. We loaded the new guns that I bought a few days prior to make sure that our slipping days were over. It had been too much bull sliding in our lane during our boosting missions, so I was making a clear way to ensure that nothing else like that occurred again.

Hearing my home phone ring loudly, I made my way to the kitchen to catch it before the caller hung up.

"Yo, who this?"

"It's me, E, Rere. I did what you asked. It worked. M.T. knows that Stanley is looking for him now, just as you asked. Is there a second part to this mission? And just to let you know, he's gonna send me an address that you're supposed to come to for him to murder you, so that's where your plan comes into effect. I hope I was of good assistance like you needed."

I took a second to reflect on what she was saying and truly appreciated the brave woman for even getting into the mix of gangsta's business. It showed the type of world we lived in today, a world where a piece of pussy could be the last thing a man spoke to before leaving.

"Yes, you helped more than you can know. He doesn't know that I'm the one who's putting this together in no type of way, correct? I'm asking for your benefit, not mines, sweetie?"

I had to be sure that this same woman wasn't running the same game back on me. The one thing I wasn't about to let take me out was moving off dumbness to fix a problem. That only led to fuckery rising higher, and I needed this to end.

"I'm sure that he doesn't know. He thinks he was being looked for by this Stanley guy the entire time. It kind of seemed like to me that he was waiting for this time to come or something. He accepted it as if he knew it was coming.

I nodded silently, knowing that she wasn't lying about it. He knew that Stanley was the only person dumb enough to shoot shots in the sunlight. That was with no repercussions to come behind it because his status was just as big.

"Thank you, ma. You did good - real good. I'll have your other two thousand dollars to you by tomorrow after everything is done. I promised Diego not to get you hurt in any kind of way, so from this point on, you have no more agenda with this mission. Understood?" I asked to be sure me and her had an agreement.

“Loud and clear, captain."

“Cool. I’ll speak to you in a li’l while,” I responded, hanging up the line.

Taking a minute to ponder to myself in the kitchen, I thought about what had to happen. It was what I waited for, and I knew for a fact that it was too late to turn back. Even after all the shit I’d been through in Athens, none of it could replace my homie’s life. Andre was a big piece of my hear, a piece that showed me how to move in the streets before I knew how to move period. Since his death, my heart had been at a standstill with the trust level and working streak. The momentum was dead without his energy, and to make it clear, he was literally the main life of my crew. My next boost was a local jewelry store located on the north side of Athens, the suburbs. I didn’t need any distractions coming my way, so the business with this was about to be addressed off hand.

I walked back into the living room. Stacy peeped my changed facial expression and stopped what he was doing. “What’s wrong, bro? Is everything all good?"

I gathered my words correctly before I answered to see how the boys were gonna take what I had to say because in the end, I was gonna need their help.

“Nah, it ain’t.”

Sky Dog slowly rose to his feet from the chair with a blank face. “Who the fuck did it, and why haven’t they been came forward, and if we know now, why are we still sitting here?" he asked with no cut.

“Because it’s not that we weren’t prepared. The problem is who we have to handle for committing this act. M.T.” I broke the news looking for all of their reactions.

The room filled with silence for a second too long, and Stacy was true first to break it.

“I don’t think we got the money or manpower to go fucking with buddy. I mean, why in the fuck would M.T. murder Andre? I don’t see any cause here. Or am I the only one thinking about this?" he said more in fear than anything.

“I don’t give a fuck what you say. If Elmadi said he did it, nigga, he did it. Period. Now how are we about to handle it?"

“I understand completely on how you feel, Stacy, but if I’m telling you this, it’s for a reason, and it’s also because I know. I’ve been following this dude around, adding up all his fuckery and bullshit since Andre was murdered, and all the points fall in accord. Now I don’t know if you think this nigga is a supernatural being or alien, but he isn’t. He’s human, and he bleeds like us. So I’ll put it this way. If you’re not ready to step with us, you can leave and stay behind. But my mind is made on what’s next for me. Anybody disagree, just get up and walk away from the table now,” I said to all my closest friends that were raised up with me. There was no reason to mask what was on the table, and I needed to see who was truly standing with me through whatever.

BoRat stood up first, slapping a clip into the .45 automatic handgun. “I’m with whatever you with, E, fuck it. This shit for Andre."

I rolled my eyes over to Sky Dog, and he nodded with a silent approval. I knew that he was more than anxious to handle some work.

I turned my head to Stacy. He looked up in my eyes unwittingly and replied, “Yeah, I’m down.”

I could hear the unsureness in his voice, and that alone let me knew at that moment to keep my eyes on him from that point on.

Picking up one of the Glocks from the table, I racked the chamber back. “It’s settled. M.T. gotta be addressed, and we about to be the ones that come forward to do it.”

“When?” Sky Dog asked impatiently.

I smirked at the gun in my hand before replying.

“Tomorrow!"

Thinking about avenging Andre’s death, I smiled. It wasn’t because of me going against the nastiest nigga in my city. It was the fact that my nigga didn’t die in vain. I just didn’t know my plan for taking him out would go totally different than I thought. Chaos was about to erupt out in Classic City, and it was all gonna be because of me.

* * *

To Be Continued...
Classic City 2
Eastside vs. Westside

Lock Down Publications and Ca$h Presents assisted publishing packages.

BASIC PACKAGE $499
Editing
Cover Design
Formatting

UPGRADED PACKAGE $800
Typing
Editing
Cover Design
Formatting

ADVANCE PACKAGE $1,200
Typing
Editing
Cover Design
Formatting
Copyright registration
Proofreading
Upload book to Amazon

LDP SUPREME PACKAGE $1,500
Typing
Editing
Cover Design
Formatting
Copyright registration
Proofreading
Set up Amazon account

Upload book to Amazon
Advertise on LDP Amazon and Facebook page

***Other services available upon request. Additional charges may apply

Lock Down Publications
P.O. Box 944
Stockbridge, GA 30281-9998
Phone # 470 303-9761

Submission Guideline

Submit the first three chapters of your completed manuscript to ldpsubmissions@gmail.com, subject line: Your book's title. The manuscript must be in a .doc file and sent as an attachment. Document should be in Times New Roman, double spaced and in size 12 font. Also, provide your synopsis and full contact information. If sending multiple submissions, they must each be in a separate email.

Have a story but no way to send it electronically? You can still submit to LDP/Ca$h Presents. Send in the first three chapters, written or typed, of your completed manuscript to:

LDP: Submissions Dept
Po Box 944
Stockbridge, Ga 30281

DO NOT send original manuscript. Must be a duplicate.

Provide your synopsis and a cover letter containing your full contact information.

Thanks for considering LDP and Ca$h Presents.

NEW RELEASES

PROTÉGÉ OF A LEGEND by COREY ROBINSON
STRAIGHT BEAST MODE 2 by DE'KARI
ANGEL 3 by ANTHONY FIELDS
CLASSIC CITY by CHRIS GREEN

Coming Soon from Lock Down Publications/Ca$h Presents

BLOOD OF A BOSS **VI**

SHADOWS OF THE GAME II

TRAP BASTARD II

By **Askari**

LOYAL TO THE GAME **IV**

By **T.J. & Jelissa**

TRUE SAVAGE **VIII**

MIDNIGHT CARTEL IV

DOPE BOY MAGIC IV

CITY OF KINGZ III

NIGHTMARE ON SILENT AVE II

THE PLUG OF LIL MEXICO II

CLASSIC CITY II

By **Chris Green**

BLAST FOR ME **III**

A SAVAGE DOPEBOY III

CUTTHROAT MAFIA III

DUFFLE BAG CARTEL VII

HEARTLESS GOON VI

By **Ghost**

A HUSTLER'S DECEIT III

KILL ZONE II

BAE BELONGS TO ME III

By **Aryanna**

KING OF THE TRAP III

By **T.J. Edwards**

GORILLAZ IN THE BAY V

3X KRAZY III

STRAIGHT BEAST MODE III

De'Kari

KINGPIN KILLAZ IV

STREET KINGS III

PAID IN BLOOD III

CARTEL KILLAZ IV

DOPE GODS III

Hood Rich

SINS OF A HUSTLA II

ASAD

RICH $AVAGE II

By Martell Troublesome Bolden

YAYO V

Bred In The Game 2

S. Allen

CREAM III

THE STREETS WILL TALK II

By Yolanda Moore

SON OF A DOPE FIEND III

HEAVEN GOT A GHETTO II

By Renta

LOYALTY AIN'T PROMISED III

By Keith Williams

I'M NOTHING WITHOUT HIS LOVE II

SINS OF A THUG II

TO THE THUG I LOVED BEFORE II

IN A HUSTLER I TRUST II

By Monet Dragun

QUIET MONEY IV

EXTENDED CLIP III

THUG LIFE IV

By **Trai'Quan**

THE STREETS MADE ME IV

By **Larry D. Wright**

IF YOU CROSS ME ONCE II

ANGEL IV

By **Anthony Fields**

THE STREETS WILL NEVER CLOSE IV

By K'ajji

HARD AND RUTHLESS III

KILLA KOUNTY III

By Khufu

MONEY GAME III

By Smoove Dolla

JACK BOYS VS DOPE BOYS II

A GANGSTA'S QUR'AN V

COKE GIRLZ II

By Romell Tukes

MURDA WAS THE CASE II

Elijah R. Freeman

THE STREETS NEVER LET GO II

By Robert Baptiste

AN UNFORESEEN LOVE III

By **Meesha**

KING OF THE TRENCHES III
by **GHOST & TRANAY ADAMS**

MONEY MAFIA II

LOYAL TO THE SOIL III

By **Jibril Williams**

QUEEN OF THE ZOO II

By **Black Migo**

VICIOUS LOYALTY III

By Kingpen

A GANGSTA'S PAIN III

By J-Blunt

CONFESSIONS OF A JACKBOY III

By Nicholas Lock

GRIMEY WAYS II

By Ray Vinci

KING KILLA II

By Vincent "Vitto" Holloway

BETRAYAL OF A THUG II

By Fre$h

THE MURDER QUEENS II

By Michael Gallon

THE BIRTH OF A GANGSTER II

By Delmont Player

TREAL LOVE II

By Le'Monica Jackson

FOR THE LOVE OF BLOOD II

By Jamel Mitchell

RAN OFF ON DA PLUG II

By Paper Boi Rari

HOOD CONSIGLIERE II

By Keese

PRETTY GIRLS DO NASTY THINGS II

By Nicole Goosby

PROTÉGÉ OF A LEGEND II

By Corey Robinson

Available Now

RESTRAINING ORDER **I & II**

By **CA$H & Coffee**

LOVE KNOWS NO BOUNDARIES **I II & III**

By **Coffee**

RAISED AS A GOON I, II, III & IV

BRED BY THE SLUMS I, II, III

BLAST FOR ME I & II

ROTTEN TO THE CORE I II III

A BRONX TALE I, II, III

DUFFLE BAG CARTEL I II III IV V VI

HEARTLESS GOON I II III IV V

A SAVAGE DOPEBOY I II

DRUG LORDS I II III

CUTTHROAT MAFIA I II

KING OF THE TRENCHES

By **Ghost**

LAY IT DOWN **I & II**

LAST OF A DYING BREED I II

BLOOD STAINS OF A SHOTTA I & II III

By **Jamaica**

LOYAL TO THE GAME I II III

LIFE OF SIN I, II III

By **TJ & Jelissa**

BLOODY COMMAS I & II

SKI MASK CARTEL I II & III

KING OF NEW YORK I II,III IV V

RISE TO POWER I II III

COKE KINGS I II III IV V

BORN HEARTLESS I II III IV

KING OF THE TRAP I II

By **T.J. Edwards**

IF LOVING HIM IS WRONG…I & II

LOVE ME EVEN WHEN IT HURTS I II III

By **Jelissa**

WHEN THE STREETS CLAP BACK I & II III

THE HEART OF A SAVAGE I II III

MONEY MAFIA

LOYAL TO THE SOIL I II

By **Jibril Williams**

A DISTINGUISHED THUG STOLE MY HEART I II & III

LOVE SHOULDN'T HURT I II III IV

RENEGADE BOYS I II III IV

PAID IN KARMA I II III

SAVAGE STORMS I II III

AN UNFORESEEN LOVE I II

By **Meesha**

A GANGSTER'S CODE I &, II III

A GANGSTER'S SYN I II III

THE SAVAGE LIFE I II III

CHAINED TO THE STREETS I II III

BLOOD ON THE MONEY I II III

A GANGSTA'S PAIN I II

By J-Blunt

PUSH IT TO THE LIMIT

By **Bre' Hayes**

BLOOD OF A BOSS **I, II, III, IV, V**

SHADOWS OF THE GAME

TRAP BASTARD

By **Askari**

THE STREETS BLEED MURDER **I, II & III**

THE HEART OF A GANGSTA I II& III

By **Jerry Jackson**

CUM FOR ME I II III IV V VI VII VIII

An **LDP Erotica Collaboration**

BRIDE OF A HUSTLA **I II & II**

THE FETTI GIRLS **I, II& III**

CORRUPTED BY A GANGSTA I, II III, IV

BLINDED BY HIS LOVE

THE PRICE YOU PAY FOR LOVE I, II ,III

DOPE GIRL MAGIC I II III

By **Destiny Skai**

WHEN A GOOD GIRL GOES BAD

By **Adrienne**

THE COST OF LOYALTY I II III

By Kweli

A GANGSTER'S REVENGE **I II III & IV**

THE BOSS MAN'S DAUGHTERS I II III IV V

A SAVAGE LOVE **I & II**

BAE BELONGS TO ME I II

A HUSTLER'S DECEIT I, II, III

WHAT BAD BITCHES DO I, II, III

SOUL OF A MONSTER I II III

KILL ZONE

A DOPE BOY'S QUEEN I II III

By **Aryanna**

A KINGPIN'S AMBITON

A KINGPIN'S AMBITION **II**

I MURDER FOR THE DOUGH

By **Ambitious**

TRUE SAVAGE I II III IV V VI VII

DOPE BOY MAGIC I, II, III

MIDNIGHT CARTEL I II III

CITY OF KINGZ I II

NIGHTMARE ON SILENT AVE

THE PLUG OF LIL MEXICO II

CLASSIC CITY

By **Chris Green**

A DOPEBOY'S PRAYER

By **Eddie "Wolf" Lee**

THE KING CARTEL **I, II & III**

By **Frank Gresham**

THESE NIGGAS AIN'T LOYAL **I, II & III**

By **Nikki Tee**

GANGSTA SHYT **I II &III**

By **CATO**

THE ULTIMATE BETRAYAL

By **Phoenix**

BOSS'N UP **I , II & III**

By **Royal Nicole**

I LOVE YOU TO DEATH

By **Destiny J**

I RIDE FOR MY HITTA

I STILL RIDE FOR MY HITTA

By **Misty Holt**

LOVE & CHASIN' PAPER

By **Qay Crockett**

TO DIE IN VAIN

SINS OF A HUSTLA

By **ASAD**

BROOKLYN HUSTLAZ

By **Boogsy Morina**

BROOKLYN ON LOCK I & II

By **Sonovia**

GANGSTA CITY

By **Teddy Duke**

A DRUG KING AND HIS DIAMOND I & II III

A DOPEMAN'S RICHES

HER MAN, MINE'S TOO I, II

CASH MONEY HO'S

THE WIFEY I USED TO BE I II

PRETTY GIRLS DO NASTY THINGS

By Nicole Goosby

TRAPHOUSE KING **I II & III**

KINGPIN KILLAZ I II III

STREET KINGS I II

PAID IN BLOOD **I II**

CARTEL KILLAZ I II III

DOPE GODS I II

By **Hood Rich**

LIPSTICK KILLAH **I, II, III**

CRIME OF PASSION I II & III

FRIEND OR FOE I II III

By **Mimi**

STEADY MOBBN' **I, II, III**

THE STREETS STAINED MY SOUL I II III

By **Marcellus Allen**

WHO SHOT YA **I, II, III**

SON OF A DOPE FIEND I II

HEAVEN GOT A GHETTO

Renta

GORILLAZ IN THE BAY **I II III IV**

TEARS OF A GANGSTA I II

3X KRAZY I II

STRAIGHT BEAST MODE I II

DE'KARI

TRIGGADALE I II III

MURDAROBER WAS THE CASE

Elijah R. Freeman

GOD BLESS THE TRAPPERS I, II, III

THESE SCANDALOUS STREETS I, II, III

FEAR MY GANGSTA I, II, III IV, V

THESE STREETS DON'T LOVE NOBODY I, II

BURY ME A G I, II, III, IV, V

A GANGSTA'S EMPIRE I, II, III, IV

THE DOPEMAN'S BODYGAURD I II

THE REALEST KILLAZ I II III

THE LAST OF THE OGS I II III

Tranay Adams

THE STREETS ARE CALLING

Duquie Wilson

MARRIED TO A BOSS I II III

By Destiny Skai & Chris Green

KINGZ OF THE GAME I II III IV V VI

Playa Ray

SLAUGHTER GANG I II III

RUTHLESS HEART I II III

By Willie Slaughter

FUK SHYT

By Blakk Diamond

DON'T F#CK WITH MY HEART I II

By Linnea

ADDICTED TO THE DRAMA I II III

IN THE ARM OF HIS BOSS II

By Jamila

YAYO I II III IV

A SHOOTER'S AMBITION I II

BRED IN THE GAME

By S. Allen

TRAP GOD I II III

RICH $AVAGE

MONEY IN THE GRAVE I II III

By Martell Troublesome Bolden

FOREVER GANGSTA

GLOCKS ON SATIN SHEETS I II

By Adrian Dulan

TOE TAGZ I II III IV

LEVELS TO THIS SHYT I II

By Ah'Million

KINGPIN DREAMS I II III

RAN OFF ON DA PLUG

By Paper Boi Rari

CONFESSIONS OF A GANGSTA I II III IV

CONFESSIONS OF A JACKBOY I II

By Nicholas Lock

I'M NOTHING WITHOUT HIS LOVE

SINS OF A THUG

TO THE THUG I LOVED BEFORE

A GANGSTA SAVED XMAS

IN A HUSTLER I TRUST

By Monet Dragun

CAUGHT UP IN THE LIFE I II III

THE STREETS NEVER LET GO

By Robert Baptiste

NEW TO THE GAME I II III

MONEY, MURDER & MEMORIES I II III

By **Malik D. Rice**

LIFE OF A SAVAGE I II III

A GANGSTA'S QUR'AN I II III IV

MURDA SEASON I II III

GANGLAND CARTEL I II III

CHI'RAQ GANGSTAS I II III

KILLERS ON ELM STREET I II III

JACK BOYZ N DA BRONX I II III

A DOPEBOY'S DREAM I II III

JACK BOYS VS DOPE BOYS

COKE GIRLZ

By Romell Tukes

LOYALTY AIN'T PROMISED I II

By Keith Williams

QUIET MONEY I II III

THUG LIFE I II III

EXTENDED CLIP I II

By **Trai'Quan**

THE STREETS MADE ME I II III

By **Larry D. Wright**

THE ULTIMATE SACRIFICE I, II, III, IV, V, VI

KHADIFI

IF YOU CROSS ME ONCE

ANGEL I II III

IN THE BLINK OF AN EYE

By **Anthony Fields**

THE LIFE OF A HOOD STAR

By Ca$h & Rashia Wilson

THE STREETS WILL NEVER CLOSE I II III

By K'ajji

CREAM I II

THE STREETS WILL TALK

By Yolanda Moore

NIGHTMARES OF A HUSTLA I II III

By King Dream

CONCRETE KILLA I II III

VICIOUS LOYALTY I II

By Kingpen

HARD AND RUTHLESS I II

MOB TOWN 251

THE BILLIONAIRE BENTLEYS I II III

By Von Diesel

GHOST MOB

Stilloan Robinson

MOB TIES I II III IV V VI

By SayNoMore

BODYMORE MURDERLAND I II III

THE BIRTH OF A GANGSTER

By Delmont Player

FOR THE LOVE OF A BOSS

By C. D. Blue

MOBBED UP I II III IV

THE BRICK MAN I II III IV

THE COCAINE PRINCESS I II III IV V

By King Rio

KILLA KOUNTY I II III

By Khufu

MONEY GAME I II

By Smoove Dolla

A GANGSTA'S KARMA I II

By FLAME

KING OF THE TRENCHES I II

by **GHOST & TRANAY ADAMS**

QUEEN OF THE ZOO

By **Black Migo**

GRIMEY WAYS

By Ray Vinci

XMAS WITH AN ATL SHOOTER

By Ca$h & Destiny Skai

KING KILLA

By Vincent "Vitto" Holloway

BETRAYAL OF A THUG

By Fre$h

THE MURDER QUEENS

By Michael Gallon

TREAL LOVE

By Le'Monica Jackson

FOR THE LOVE OF BLOOD

By Jamel Mitchell

HOOD CONSIGLIERE

By Keese

PROTÉGÉ OF A LEGEND

By Corey Robinson

BOOKS BY LDP'S CEO, CA$H

TRUST IN NO MAN

TRUST IN NO MAN 2

TRUST IN NO MAN 3

BONDED BY BLOOD

SHORTY GOT A THUG

THUGS CRY

THUGS CRY 2

THUGS CRY 3

TRUST NO BITCH

TRUST NO BITCH 2

TRUST NO BITCH 3

TIL MY CASKET DROPS

RESTRAINING ORDER

RESTRAINING ORDER 2

IN LOVE WITH A CONVICT

LIFE OF A HOOD STAR

XMAS WITH AN ATL SHOOTER

CPSIA information can be obtained
at www.ICGtesting.com
Printed in the USA
LVHW081100290822
727089LV00007B/110